For ... *(handwritten inscription)*

DOGWOOD SEASON

Michael Altieri *(signature)*

Michael Altieri

PublishAmerica
Baltimore

ISBN: 1-4241-3945-7
PUBLISHED BY PUBLISHAMERICA, LLLP
www.publishamerica.com
Baltimore

Printed in the United States of America

Acknowledgments

I would like to thank my wife Gina for never questioning my need or desire to write this novel. She spent many a lonely night while I banged away on the computer, never once complaining. When I suggested I might not finish it, she encouraged me to continue.

CHAPTER 1

"Corrino, where's Gianni?" Lieutenant Nelson shouted, his voice trembling with excitement.

The same eerie anxiousness showered Detective Corrino as she reminisced about the day the lieutenant introduced her to the squad as a new detective, back in 2000. She learned shortly after that day, that if she wanted to fit in, she had to play the game. She had to be accepted as an equal, as a detective, not as the female detective.

"It's not my turn to watch him, Lieutenant," Brenda replied, seriously as she could, fighting off a smirk. "Did you check the little boys' room?"

Other detectives were going about their business while smothering smirks and snickers, as the lieutenant continued scanning the second floor room that housed the Fairfield Police Department Detective Bureau, for Detective Frank Gianni.

He was dressed in a minimalist three-piece gray pinstriped suit looking neat and polished as usual, always offering an aurora of confidence despite his personal problems. Lieutenant Nelson didn't need any shit from Detective Corrino today. He hasn't been sleeping well these days. Not since his third divorce was finalized last week.

The first wife was the best one, but he always put the job first and his family second. He wanted to be promoted to captain, and you can't get there if you don't make the job your number-one priority. So he lost his wife and daughter to the job, with his wife remarrying a few years later and relocating to the west coast.

His second wife was fifteen years younger than him and a real knock out. She was a beautiful, blue-eyed blond with looks that could kill and a body to match her sexy style. She belonged in Hollywood he would tell her, not with him. She could have had her pick but she really got off on being married to a cop. The more dangerous his assignments the amorous she would become. During one investigation that involved some undercover work dealing drugs, she was convinced that he'd surely be killed. When he returned home alive and unharmed, she couldn't get enough of him. They spent the next two days in bed screwing their brains out. Then one day he came home to a note saying that she decided their marriage was too stressful for her and she was filing for a divorce. There wasn't a rhyme or reason to explain that one. So his perfect marriage was over, just like that. The job continued as though everything was coming up roses in his life.

Now at fifty-five, his third marriage has ended in the toilet as well, and this time within the first year. Her name was Mandy and she used to strip in a New York City club that he began to frequent, while drinking away his troubles. She was a great dancer with a body toned to perfection. She sported that over the top look that the lieutenant always felt made her look like a Playboy model and that was the main attraction. She had a great derriere to compliment her 40 DD-23-36 figure. She confessed to him that before they met she often prostituted herself when she needed money to buy dope. But he didn't care about her past. He didn't care who she did as long as she was only doing him now.

He wanted to take care of her. He was in love and wanted to help her continue to stay straight, even though she didn't think she needed his help. He would have done practically anything to help her stay on track. He really loved her and she loved him too. She was a reformed junky, except she didn't stay reformed for very long. The love affair with crack was stronger. Soon she was back to her old friends and once again turning tricks for drug money. That's why she became a stripper in the first place. She could make plenty of money to support her habit. So she thought, but eventually the drug habit became too expensive and the toll on her body to extensive. So she started offering sexual favors while waiting for her turn to perform. Eventually she got fired because she would show up high as a kite and her performance would lack concupiscence. Strippers need to draw men into their little world of illusion. The longer the patrons are locked in the longer they stay and drink. The club could not survive without steady returning customers. Breasts and asses can become boring to the average man if paraded without substance. The cocaine lent itself to sexy kinky dancing, but the blank look on her face didn't allow eye contact. Thus the fantasy dies.

Since she couldn't afford to pay the dealer fifty dollars a day without the lieutenant getting suspicious, she decided she would spend a day or two a week being his whore and letting him pimp her around too. She would end up with enough cocaine to last her a week or more. Eventually she got caught up in a police sting and got busted for prostitution. She thought they would let her go when she told them her husband was Lieutenant Nelson. But it turned out the detective on the scene had a confrontation with Nelson years ago when they both were detectives in neighboring Bridgeport. So instead of a deal, he made sure that the charges would stand up in court and the news spread throughout the police department and political arena like fire. Agonizing embarrassment reined upon Lieutenant Nelson, leaving him no choice but to immediately file for divorce.

If Brenda Corrino was a man he would've told her to go fuck herself, but he knows he can't say that these days. *Too many damn women in the police force these days.* He's seen too many men passed up for detective positions because of equal rights bullshit and that really pissed him off.

"Sit on it, Corrino," Lieutenant Nelson barked as he headed for the men's bathroom.

Pushing open the door he's greeted by a toilet flushing, causing Brenda and a few other detectives to crack up laughing. "Frank, you in here?" asked the lieutenant as the door closed behind him.

"What the fuck?" Frank snapped. "A guy can't even take a crap in peace around here!"

Frank Gianni was a seventeen-year veteran of the Fairfield Connecticut Police Department and was raised in nearby Bridgeport. He was six feet tall with dark Italian features and a muscular body, a good-looking guy that commanded his share of attention from the felines. He was the youngest of four siblings. His brother was an attorney in New York City and his two sisters were housewives. One was happily married while the other was having an affair with her husband's brother.

He was married to Marie and had two boys and a girl. Marie was born and raised in Fairfield and met Frank before he was a cop, when he planned on being a big-shot attorney, too. Marie had plans of her own, of a pampered married life, being able to buy what she wanted, when she wanted. Three or four vacations a year without a strain on the household budget would have been good, too. At least she got to be a stay-at-home mom and raise her kids the right way.

Although Frank had planned to be an attorney just like his older brother, somewhere along the way the police bug bit him. After receiving a degree in law enforcement from the University of Bridgeport, Frank entered the police academy, graduating at the top of his class in 1986. He became a Patrolman in Fairfield in 1987 and in 1992 with encouragement from his sergeant, he took the detective's exam, receiving one of the highest scores ever achieved for a policeman with fewer than ten years of service. He'd been a detective for the past twelve years, six of those years in homicide.

Throughout his young career Frank solved many difficult cases and had expected a swift promotion to Lieutenant. However he'd been passed over several times because some of his superiors thought he was a showoff who often solved murders by luck, even though other detectives aren't able to solve them. A few of his coworkers respected his ability, while most thought he was just plain lucky and too damn cocky for his own good. His partner thought he was an extraordinary detective.

During his first year as a detective, Frank was put to the test while learning the ropes with seasoned partner, Joe McLaughlin, on a string of burglaries. Joe only had a few years to retirement and he welcomed having a young partner. Someone young to chase the assholes through the yards and jump the twelve-foot-high fences often found in the well-to-do neighborhoods was an appreciated addition. He was someone to muscle the suspects when required, someone quick with good eyesight to watch his back. Joe figured it was a fair exchange to keep his name out of the obituary column. With Joe's experience to rely on, Frank was able to determine that the same person was committing all the robberies. Others working on the case weren't so sure and they went out of their way to prove that the rookie detective was wrong. As it turned out, Frank was right, and Joe insisted on giving all the credit to Frank.

The following year there was a rapist to contend with in the affluent Greenfield Hill section of Fairfield. The area was well known throughout Connecticut for its large spectacular expensive homes and well to do people. It is home to many celebrities who work in neighboring New York City. The famous Dogwood Festival is held each May in Greenfield Hill and it was hardly the place you would expect a rapist to prosper. The rapist was working an area where many new homes had been built in the past three years. This particular rapist liked to prey on the young, spoiled housewives in the morning, in their homes, after they've seen their children off to school. Since Frank had recently moved his family to Fairfield from Bridgeport, this case hit home. He had a great-looking housewife of his own to worry about and decided he would have to solve this one fast. Once the third rape was reported and it was established that they were dealing with a serial rapist, Frank solved the crime and caught the bastard before he could rape again. Frank had a gift for talking to the victims and getting them to reveal information that they subconsciously suppressed.

The rapist thought he was smart, wearing a condom when he raped his victims, knowing the DNA from his semen could get him caught. He was also completely shaven from head to toe so that he wouldn't leave any hair samples on the victims or their beds. Frank and Joe were at a standstill, waiting for the rapist to strike again, when Frank began to think about some of the case studies from the police academy. Most rapists are out to humiliate their victims. Rape was bad enough, but what about sodomy or oral sex. He remembered in several of the case studies that the women were forced to give oral sex before they were raped. The

DNA evidence from their mouths' was enough to get a conviction. Yet none of these three victims indicated that anything other than intercourse had occurred.

Frank returned to the latest victim, Mrs. Adams, and persuaded her to tell him the story once again from the beginning. She was your average thirty something Greenfield Hill housewife, an attractive slim brunette with a husband and a couple of kids. Her husband made six figures and she spent it pretty fast. They had a spacious, four- thousand-square foot home and a couple of acres of land. Her world was close to perfect until the rape three days earlier. She told him how she was standing at the kitchen sink, rinsing the breakfast dishes to put them into the dishwasher when she sensed someone standing behind her. She was still wearing the terrycloth robe she always wore while making the kids breakfast and sending them off to school. As she turned around, she was punched in the face and knocked silly. The rapist dragged her into her bedroom while she tried to regain her senses. He pulled off her robe and threw her onto the bed, as she desperately tried to make sense of what was happening. She began to come to her senses as this strange black hairless man straddled her head, dangling his big hard penis in her face, slapping her with it, as though trying to wake her out of her stupor.

Frank jumped right in saying, "Was that when he made you take it in your mouth?"

"No...no," she cried out.... "That didn't happen to me."

Frank asked, "Did he ejaculate in your mouth?"

Now the victim began crying uncontrollably and Joe was pulling Frank back. "That's enough Frank," Joe shouted as he tried to corral Frank. "Hasn't she been through enough? She doesn't need to relive the rape all over again Frank," Joe continued to argue.

Frank kept his cool and put his arms around her, hugging her firmly. "It's okay. You don't have to tell me anything that you don't want to tell me. I'll just wait until the bastard rapes another young woman to find out if he forces her to pleasure him orally," Frank whispered into her ear. "If that happens, we'll have a better chance of catching the bastard and stopping him from hurting anybody else."

Mrs. Adams continued to sob softly into Frank's shoulder, holding on to him with desperation. Frank could feel his shirt was absorbing her tears. After what seemed like an eternity to Joe, she whispered into Frank's ear.

"The rapist tied my hands to the headboard with his belt and he put it in my mouth. He pushed his penis in and out as I lay motionless, trying to block out what was happening to me. I sensed that he was getting excited as his penis grew larger, and I was afraid that he was going to…you know, ejaculate in my mouth. My husband is not to be told about that part. Do you understand? Never!" Mrs. Adams cried out, now on the brink of hysteria. "Otherwise I'll deny it ever happened!"

Frank hugged her quivering body even tighter as he softly encouraged her to continue. "If your husband finds out it will only be because you told him," Frank spoke softly into her long brown hair.

She began to speak again. "He finally pulled it out of my mouth, after what seemed like an eternity, and for a moment I thought maybe he'd leave me alone. Maybe he had his thrill. Instead the bastard took out a condom and put it on right in front of my face, smiling as he talked to me. How would you like it today, up the ass? Is that the way you like your husband to give it to you? Yeah, I bet you'd like me to fuck your ass, wouldn't you? All the time he's smiling at me. Then he put his finger in my rear," she sobbed softly. "I knew I was going to be sodomized because he seemed to be getting great pleasure from fingering me. I started to cry, begging him; 'Please don't hurt me,' I said.

"'Today's your lucky day,' he said grinning from ear to ear.

"'Please leave me alone, my kids will be home soon,' I pleaded into his deaf ears.

"'He rubbed his penis on my face after he got the condom on. and he shrugged his shoulders and said, 'See, no lube on this condom.'

"I braced myself for the worse when suddenly without warning he pulled away and shoved it into my vagina, violently rapping me, quickly groaning with disgusting gratification. Then, just like that it was over. He pulled up his pants and released my hands from his belt. While putting on his belt he warned me to just lie there and keep my mouth shut until he was out of the neighborhood. He said if I called the cops he'd come back and beat me up," she recanted as tears slowly rolled down her face. "He said he'd rape me in front of my children." Pulling away from Detective Gianni, she walked over to the window, staring out into the bright delicate sunshine, the buds of a young dogwood tree she planted after the birth of her last child, staring back at her. "It's almost dogwood season you know. How could such a thing happen in this beautiful peaceful neighborhood?" Neither the tree nor the detectives offered any answers.

The police report indicated that she didn't shower until after the hospital examined her and they took samples for DNA testing from her. She refused to allow them to swab her mouth because she insisted that he didn't kiss her or penetrate her mouth.

Frank gave her a few minutes to compose herself as he contemplated his approach to the next round of questions. She had given him more details than he expected and for the first time he felt like he really understood the horror that rape victims experience. Frank just had one more very tough answer to get from Mrs. Adams. He walked over to where she was standing, careful not to get to close. "After he raped you and fled, what was the first thing you did?" Frank asked.

"I grabbed a tissue and spit," she cried out, "then I flushed it down the toilet. Then I grabbed some mouthwash and gargled."

Frank's heart sank realizing that any possible DNA evidence was gone. He knew that most men pre-ejaculate during sexual stimulation and that would have been more than enough DNA evidence to use for a conviction.

"No...wait, I was going to go into the bathroom to flush it but I heard a noise and I thought he was coming back so I threw it in the pail in my bedroom and locked the door."

Joe jumped up and ran into the master bedroom, only to find an empty pail. "It's empty, Frank," Joe said as he returned to the living room.

"What day does the city pick up the trash here, Mrs. Adams?" Frank asked.

"Friday," Mrs. Adams replied.

"That's today," screamed Joe as he ran out the front door.

Luckily it hadn't been picked up yet. They took all the trash with them for analysis and to make a long story short, a DNA match was made to a convicted rapist, released from prison a few months earlier. His parole officer was contacted for his address and the rest was history. Frank received all kinds of press and made an appearance on the Good Morning Connecticut television show. The police commissioner requested that Frank be appointed homicide detective, and it was announced at Joe McLaughlin's retirement party. Frank worked alone for several months until Brenda Corrino got promoted to detective and the lieutenant made them partners. He didn't love having a female partner but he didn't hate it as much as the lieutenant had hoped he would.

"I just got a call from the Easton P.D., Frank," continued Lieutenant Nelson. "There's been a murder at Lake Mohegan. A rookie cop from Easton, out with his family on his day off, made the discovery. He called his lieutenant saying that this was an unusual murder, perhaps an actress, and he didn't think it was a good idea to just call 911."

"Damn rookies," moaned Frank, "a body's a body. He probably never saw a dead body before except for a fucking funeral. He just jumps to the conclusion that it's a murder," replied Frank, as the stall door swung open. He held his pants from falling as he headed for the sink. He struggled to see himself clearly in the cheap mirror as he washed his hands, holding his pants up with his legs spread out at the knees. Pulling up his pants as he tucked in his shirt and straightened out his favorite Jerry Garcia tie, he glanced back at the lieutenant, hoping he had left and dumped this case on someone else.

"The body was actually found on the Fairfield side of the lake. The captain suggested that I assign this one to you, Frank. Take a ride over there and take a look. If it looks like bullshit I'll reassign it. The victim was a female in her twenties according to the rookie, and he thinks she might be somebody special because she looked familiar to him. Take Corrino up there with you. Maybe she'll pick up on some female stuff."

"Yeah, maybe she'll be able to tell me if the victim has two tits and an ass," Frank said, laughing as he headed for the door. Lieutenant Nelson burst into laughter too, causing Frank to laugh even harder as they pulled open the door.

"Hey, Brenda," Frank said louder than was necessary. "The lieutenant thinks you can teach me a few things about the female body. Think you can handle it?"

Lieutenant Nelson quickly retreated to his office to avoid being caught in the middle.

Before she could answer, one of the other detectives made an outline of a big pair of boobs in front of his chest and started strutting around like a two-bit whore. Once again the room filled with laughter.

"I can handle you with two fingers Frank," she replied with a grin while holding up the thumb and first finger of her right hand, slightly jerking it up and down, "but you're beyond teaching, Frank."

"Up yours!" Frank snapped back.

"You know, Frank," Brenda continued, "if it was politically correct, I'd tell you and the lieutenant to go fuck yourselves." Brenda glowed with victory as she circulated among the other detectives, grinning from ear to ear, picking up a few high fives along the way, basking in the glory of ending up with the upper hand. "But I can't say that now, can I?"

"Let's go," Frank yelled, obviously pissed off at everybody in the room. "The lieutenant wants us to check out a possible homicide at Lake Mohegan."

CHAPTER 2

Brenda sat on the passenger side as usual. *Like I didn't take the same high-speed drivers training that all police officers take at the academy.* Female cops were still treated like second-rate citizens within the police department. Although she scored very high grades on the detective's exam and was the youngest female to be promoted to detective, she couldn't gain the respect of the male cops, not even her own partner. Brenda was a very attractive blue-eyed redhead that men didn't get tired of looking at. Most people didn't look beyond her beauty to see that she was very intelligent and an excellent detective. At 5 foot 8 inches and one hundred and thirty pounds, with all the curves in the right places, her intelligence was usually the last thing to be noticed or remembered.

She joined the Fairfield Police Department in 1998, fresh out of the police academy after earning a four-year degree in criminal justice from Fairfield University. Before that she attended a conservatory, did some modeling, and even landed a few television commercials and bit parts. But the drugs, booze, and wild life didn't sit well with her. She needed more than a facade for a life. She needed something she could sink her heart and soul into and one day her boyfriend suggested she become an attorney. So she decided to take a few college law courses and soon realized that she wanted to enforce the laws, not defend them. She was ambitious and tenacious to become Fairfield's first female police captain and would do whatever it took to get her there.

Although she hated herself for it, she did use her sex appeal to help her get promoted as the first female homicide detective in the Fairfield Police Department. Within two years after being promoted to detective, she was appointed to homicide. She would have gotten there eventually, but with a little flirting and a few dinner dates with the right people, she cut about eight years off the wait. She didn't sleep her way up the ladder or anything, but she did make herself available to date people that could help her achieve her goals. She gave away a little milk, too, but never the whole cow.

Frank worked alone after Joe McLaughlin retired until Brenda's boosterism moved her into homicide. He didn't appreciate how she got there but gave her credit for finding a way to achieve her goal. He didn't love having a female partner but he didn't hate it either. At least he was the senior partner and she was easy on the eyes. Yeah, real easy on the eyes. Too damn easy on the eyes. Fairfield was home to many celebrities and rich rebuilt bitches, yet those women had nothing over Brenda Corrino.

The Town of Fairfield was located in southwestern Connecticut on the coast of Long Island Sound, approximately sixty miles from New York City. Fairfield had a population of about fifty-eight thousand residents settled into an area of about thirty square miles. The Fairfield Police Department was located south of Interstate 95 and south of the Post Road, at 100 Reef

Road. Currently, there were more than one hundred full-time police officers on the force.

The majority of small retailers were located in this area, mostly on the Post Road, also known as Route One. I guess you could say that this was Fairfield's downtown. The majority of these businesses relied on the locals who loved their coffee shops, restaurants, and exclusive jewelry and clothing stores. Many medical office buildings scattered throughout the area helped to bolster business from the surrounding towns and cities.

There wasn't an easy way to get to Lake Mohegan from Reef Road because it was tucked away up in the northeast corner of Fairfield, bordered by Easton and Bridgeport. They could have taken the scenic route up North Benson Road but since it wasn't rush hour, they took Interstate 95 for a few miles, getting off at the Black Rock Turnpike exit. Heading north, you found the other major retail area along Black Rock Turnpike, consisting mostly of strip malls, many with chain stores, and they also had their share of medical offices, too. Black Rock Turnpike was just as busy as the Post Road because as it continued further up towards Easton it intersected with Route 15, the Merritt Parkway. Because of the two major highways, many Fairfield residents work in nearby New York City.

A right turn onto Fairfield Woods Road put you back into the residential area again. The homes in this area were older and smaller than many Fairfield homes. Then a left onto Morehouse Highway, the road that took you to Lake Mohegan.

"Why are you doing that?" Frank asked. "You don't need makeup to examine a murder scene."

"I'm not getting any younger, Frank," she said as she continued to apply a fresh coat of bright red lipstick.

"You're not even forty yet, are you? Besides, you're a cop. You're not supposed to look pretty!"

"I'm the same age as Marie," Brenda snapped back.

"How do you know my wife's age?"

"Are you kidding? Every time she calls and you're not around, we talk."

"About what?"

"About you, what else?" Brenda could hardly contain herself.

"Oh don't give me that crap," Frank shot back. "Marie's not that hard up for conversation. Now what's with the fucking makeup?"

"Like I said before, I'm not getting any younger. You never know when you're going to meet Mr. Right. So why shouldn't I try to look my best at all times? Besides you did say there's a dead body in the park, and that means the new medical examiner might be working this one," Brenda purred.

"Robbing the cradle aren't you?" Frank asked with a smile.

"What, are you jealous?" Brenda shouted.

Frank rolled his eyes and softly laughed. "Why aren't you married yet? Seems to me you could get any man you want. Too damn fussy, aren't you?"

"Well, I do have some standards, but I wouldn't say I'm fussy, just cautious. I don't want to get married just to end up divorced like half the cops in America. Besides, most of the guys I date are turned off when I tell them I'm a cop. That's a long-term relationship killer. So I think I'll have to marry another cop or someone in the law enforcement field. Otherwise it's three dates and goodbye. Drinks and dinner for the first date. Then drinks, dinner and more drinks, sometimes followed by sex on the second date. The third date is no dinner, maybe drinks and always sex," Brenda said laughing at herself. "Once they stop buying me dinner, it's time to say goodbye."

They shared a laugh as Frank turned off of Morehouse Highway and into the parking lot of Lake Mohegan. A typical spring day, with brilliant sunshine and about sixty-five degrees. As he drove into the large parking lot there were kids playing, people walking their dogs, businessmen and woman enjoying their lunch, and a dead woman waiting several hundred yards away. The park wasn't actually open yet, but people still went there to enjoy the walking trails or have lunch while enjoying the view of the water. The park would officially open on May 15 for the public, but they let the fishermen use the lake at the start of the fishing season in April. Nothing seemed to faze people these days. That was a good thing because this beautiful bright day was about to turn ominous and appalling.

"You'd think with all the strobe lights flashing, yellow police tape running all over the place, and dozens of cops standing around, there would be a few curiosity seekers trying to get closer to the murder scene," Frank remarked. "Instead they're keeping their distance."

"That's Fairfield for you. I'm here to enjoy my lunch, and a murder isn't going to get in my way."

"What the hell? Why so many cops?" Frank yelled out the window towards the first uniformed officer he saw as he parked the car. His questions remained unanswered as they approached the entrance that extends access into the beach area.

Frank couldn't help the feeling he was getting about this one. *Too many cops here for one body.* Up on the hill, on a street on the other side of the lake, Frank could see police cars from neighboring Easton stopping cars entering from Easton and questioning the occupants. Morehouse road ran along side the lake and with a left and a right you would end up in Easton. No question this was a murder. And you don't waste all these cops protecting the scene unless it's a murder extraordinaire.

"Hello, Detectives," said Patrolman Ray Allen while safeguarding the entrance. Ray was a handsome young rookie with a scar on his face from a fight during his high school days. Frank had seen him in action at other crime scenes and liked the way he treated every crime scene as though the President of the United States himself were lying there dead.

"It's Ray, isn't it?" Frank asked Patrolman Allen. "Yes, sir, Detective Gianni," Patrolman Allen replied as he gave Detective Corrino a quick once over and a smile of approval. "Good afternoon, Detective," Patrolman Allen acknowledged her with the respect she deserved.

"Hi there, Ray," she replied professionally but with a flirtatious glance of approval.

"Was the gate locked when you arrived?" Frank asked.

"I didn't see a lock."

"Why do we have a three-ring circus out here?"

"I guess because it's Alana Andrews that's been murdered, and she's completely nude."

"Who?" asked Frank.

"She's a hot soap opera actress, Frank, about 23 years old," Brenda intervened. "She's been on all the talk shows lately. In fact, I read recently that she's working on a film with Tom Cruise."

Frank didn't respond. His mind was racing a mile a minute as he walked slowly over the sand, past the children's playground equipment and the lifeguard station towards the crime scene. He stopped at the water's edge, to take a broad view of the area surrounding the crime scene. Brenda trailed about ten feet behind him. Looking up towards the crime scene, a good hundred yards away, he wondered which way the murderer entered the park. He speculated that it was inconceivable that the murderer carried a dead body from the parking lot, through the gate, and up the hill over the rough terrain all that way. The lake was surrounded by a hundred and seventy acres of woodland excluding the street and parking lot. Except for the homes in plain sight on Morehouse Highway and the intersecting streets, there wasn't a house that could be seen through the denseness of the trees. *She must have been killed here.* When he reached the crime scene, he stopped and turned around, looking away towards the street at the surrounding homes. *Actresses don't live in this neighborhood.*

"Hi, Brenda," said Detective Walter Baker, ignoring Frank for a moment. "This one is kind of bizarre. Not something you're going to find very pleasant."

"How you doing, Walt?" Brenda inquired, ignoring the detective's concern. *When is murder pleasant?* "How's the Mrs.?"

"She's just fine now that she's working again," said Walt with a smile on his face. "That layoff didn't sit too well with her. You're still working with the boy wonder, I see."

"Frank's not so bad once you get to know him. He's no wonder boy, but he is a very creditable detective. So tell me, what's so uncanny about this one?"

"Better take a look for yourself," interrupted Frank. "I think it's best to get your own first impression and let your mind react with your own theory. How you doing, Walt? I heard you were having back trouble again."

"Yeah, I chased some young punk for about six blocks last week after he shot-up a liquor store on the Post Road, and I tripped over a flowerpot that some asshole thought would dress up the front of his clothing store. I went down like I was being tackled by Tedy Bruschi and screwed up my back. Maybe I can get out on a medical this time," Walt chuckled.

They all laughed knowing that the last thing Walt wanted was out. He may have slowed down a little since he turned fifty-four, but he still enjoyed the game. He added a few extra pounds onto his six-foot frame over the last ten years, too. That plus his age has caused him to slow down quite a bit. But the pursuit, capture, and conviction of a criminal are still the drugs of choice for him.

"So where's the body, Walt?" Frank inquired, growing impatient with the chit-chat bullshit that he often found to be a waste of time.

"Up over that hill," Walt replied, pointing towards a swarm of policemen. "Come on, I can't wait to hear your take on this one."

Walt led them up the hill, being careful to stay within the path that was cordoned off by police tape.

"Is the rookie who found the body still here?" asked Frank.

"No, I told him to take his wife and kid home," answered Walt. "You want to talk to him? He's not one of ours. He's with Easton. I have his phone number, home address, and work schedule for the rest of the week."

"Yeah, I'll need to talk to him," Frank replied with disgust. "He was the first person at the crime scene. Did anyone question him?"

"Well, not formally," Walt stammered. "I didn't write much down because I figured you would be questioning him anyway."

Frank didn't want to get into a pissing contest with Walt. Walt was from the old school of hard knocks and has solved many crimes over the years, and he knew better than that. He should have questioned the rookie while everything was fresh and written everything down. "Did you happen to ask him what time he discovered the body?" Frank asked trying not to be sarcastic.

"I think he said about ten thirty this morning," Walt answered as he quickly pulled out his notebook and searched for the answer on the blank paper. "Yeah, ten thirty."

"Give Brenda his name and everything. You know this kid, Walt?" Frank inquired as they closed in on the body.

"No. He's with Easton P.D. He's a rookie. I'm sure he knows not to touch anything if that's what you're wondering."

Frank didn't respond. He could see the body now.

CHAPTER 3

They exchanged pleasantries with the other police personnel as they approached the body. A strange sense of excitement filled the air. Perched up against a large tree was a beautiful Caucasian woman with blonde hair, completely naked. At a quick glance you might think she was alive, her beautiful green eyes wide open and looking straight ahead. Her voluminous shoulder-length hair appeared as though she had just returned from a hair salon. Her face had makeup and her lips were freshly painted with a bright scarlet lipstick. Her breasts pointed straight out, both nipples pierced with a gold ring. Her legs were also straight out and slightly parted. Her toenails and fingernails glistened from a fresh coat of nail polish that matched her lips. She wasn't just beautiful. She was drop-dead gorgeous. She sat there as though she was waiting for her lover to return, except her hands were tied to the tree behind her back.

"Looks like the CSI boys are finished for now," muttered Walt.

When they got up close to her they could see the gold rings

were engraved. Frank couldn't make out the engraving. The writing was much too small to be read with the naked eye.

"See if you can read what it says on these rings, Brenda," Frank said pointing to one of the nipple rings.

Before she could react Walt intervened, "It says 'bitch.' The word's etched into each one. We used a magnifying glass to read it."

"Her breasts probably have implants. They're too big to be standing at attention like that," Brenda interjected.

Protruding from the victims' mouth was a pair of rubber testicles. Brenda leaned in close, being careful not to disturb anything, and said, "Judging by that bulge in her throat, it looks like there's a rubber penis attached to those balls. I pray to God she was dead when he shoved that thing down her throat."

"The autopsy should be able to tell us," Frank answered. "Let's get her untied and see if there are any wounds on her back. That looks like painter rope. The kind of rope to tie up boats at the pier. Did we get photos of this rope and knot?" Frank yelled over to the crime scene photographer.

"The entire crime scene has been photographed, including the rope," the photographer retorted as he headed down to his car. "The Medical Examiner and the CSI team did their thing, too; otherwise you'd be disturbing evidence right now," the photographer added.

"No shit, Sherlock," Frank shouted. *Sarcastic bastard!* "You keep playing with your camera and leave the real investigate work to the people that know what they're doing. Don't take off yet. I'm in charge now, and I may want a few more pictures." *Asshole!*

Pulling out his Swiss Army pocketknife Frank cut the rope on the side so he didn't disturb the knot. Gently pulling the body forward they examined her backside for wounds. "What's that?" Frank questioned. "Looks like a little blood." Slowly turning the victim onto her side to see what was going on revealed another dildo protruding from her rectum. A small amount of blood had oozed out and stained her upper thigh.

"This sick bastard must really hate women," Brenda said strongly, trying not to show her feminine disgust.

"You better get that photographer back up here, Walt," Frank said. "I'd like to get some pictures of this before we turn her over for the autopsy. It's obvious she wasn't killed here. Did they say anything about the time of death?"

"Yeah they said it probably happened between ten and midnight last night, and she's probably been sitting out here since about three this morning," answered Walt after fumbling with his notebook.

"The killer had time to fix her makeup and hair, so she couldn't have been killed too far from here," said Frank. "It's no easy task to transport a body to this location, either."

"Walt, what about forensics? Any fingerprints or footprints?" Brenda asked.

"I don't think they found anything obvious out here or on the body. You better check with them. Hopefully the medical examiner will find some latent prints or DNA evidence when he gets her back to the shop," Walt answered. "I'm leaving. This one is all yours now."

"Okay, Walt. Say hello to the missus for me," Frank replied.

"Take it easy, Walt," Brenda added as Walt made his way down the hill, stopping to tell the photographer he was needed again.

"This has the makings of a serial killer," Frank stated.

"What the hell you talking about, Frank?" asked Brenda. "It's only one murder."

"See the way the body was posed and left out here on display so that it could easily be found? Humiliation. It's all about humiliation. He's organized, too. He takes his time to redo the victim's hair and makeup. And I'm guessing that she wasn't wearing those nipple piercings before she ran into the killer."

"Those piercings may not mean anything. That's the in thing these days for young people," said Brenda.

"They're symbols. Women are bitches. The bright red lipstick and nails. Women are whores. The medical examiner will be able to tell us when those piercings were done," answered Frank, annoyed that Brenda was questioning his reasoning. "The killer did the piercing. In fact I'll bet you lunch that the nipple jewelry and the toys were done while she was still alive. That was probably the finale of the humiliation and sexual abuse that this girl suffered. That's how these bastards get their rocks off."

"We don't know for sure that she was raped, either," Brenda countered.

"There are abrasions on her thighs and genital area, but I don't see any vaginal bleeding or semen present."

"We may not know for sure, but I'm willing to bet you a month of lunches that she was raped and probably sodomized, too. That's why the bastard put those dildos in her to show us immediately what he did. He's probably getting his rocks off again just thinking about us discovering what he did. He could be in the woods watching us right now. Tell your boyfriend he can take the body after the photographer takes the pictures, and we'll catch up with him later," Frank said while pointing towards the new young M.E. "I'll call the lieutenant and tell him to send a few people down here to help us canvas the park and the neighborhood. Maybe there were some guys fishing last night or early this morning. Sound good to you?"

"Yeah, and tell him to get us a current address and some background information. We need to know who her agent was and where he was last night," Brenda added.

"You start questioning those people that are still hanging around. I'll catch up with you in a few minutes."

Brenda headed down the hill towards the walking trail where a small group of curiosity seekers had gathered. Frank stared out into the woods observing the diversity of the trees, some areas more dense than others, wondering where and how the murderer managed to bring the body to this location. And how the murderer managed to bring the body to this location unnoticed. At least one thing was obvious. It was almost dogwood season.

CHAPTER 4

Monday 3:00 PM

"That's it…smile." *Click-whirr, click-whirr.* "Beautiful! Give me a little more cleavage this time. You know how much men enjoy cleavage, don't you, Candie?" *Click-whirr, click-whirr.* "Okay now, give me that three-quarter turn so they can see you're wearing a thong." *Click-whirr, click-whirr.* "Great! Your photos are going to be hot. Okay…I guess we're done here. We did the portraits, the formals, and the sexy bikini shots. Are you interested in doing some topless or nudes for your portfolio or personal collection?" Mark Alexander asked with routine professional smoothness.

"I don't think so. I've never taken my clothes off for the camera," Candie replied nervously. "Why should I start now?"

"Look, Candie, you're young, beautiful, and want to be an actress. If you don't think every producer and director that you read for isn't going to ask you to strip down to your birthday suit, you should pack your bags now and go home. It won't matter what part you're reading for, either. They will tell you that they need to see your body, because as other parts come up, they can easily decide if you are right for those parts. Now if you're not ready to do that, you simply submit your portfolio of beautiful nudes, properly posed and showing you at your very best. That's just show business. All those movie people are a bunch of horny bastards. All the successful actresses had to strip for their pre-audition meetings, and in the old days they even had to perform sex acts to even be considered for a part. Today there's less of that, but it still happens. Some actresses think it's the only way to break into show business. I'm just telling you this for your own good. If you're not comfortable with me taking the photos, get someone else. Just get used to being naked in front of the camera. Imagine doing a nude scene for a movie, and there are probably 30 or more people watching you do it. It doesn't matter to me, Candie. I'm just giving you some friendly advice. Get comfortable in front of a camera now so you don't go and blow your chance when you have to do it at an audition."

Candie Street wasn't the most beautiful woman Mark ever photographed, but she was definitely a hottie. With red hair down below her waist, a tight, compact rear, and a great pair of boobs, she ranked somewhere in his top twenty photographed hotties. She was svelte, and her breasts weren't large compared to many others, but based on what he'd seen so far they appeared naturally firm, no implants. He pictured Candie naked for a moment, posing just for him, looking into the camera with those big blue eyes, her firm breasts jutting straight out. *She's probably about 36 C-20-34. She'll be shy at first and afraid to turn her crouch towards the camera, but getting bolder with each click of the shutter. Maybe she'll get turned on as we work and let me have her when were done.* It's happened before but it doesn't happen often enough to satisfy him. He's photographed hundreds of beautiful women but only had sex with five. Three of them willingly, two right there on the set, and the third on a second date. He thought he should be nailing the majority of them. *After all, I'm a good-looking guy. They're such cock teasers. They let me see them naked and spread eagle, acting so damn sexy and making love to my camera…to me.* Mark shifted his body a little so that Candie wouldn't notice the bulge beginning to form in his pants. *I make them look great, better in the pics than in real life, and the least they could do is properly thank me.*

Candie studied Mark's face as she debated within herself. *Should I do the nudes? Sure sounds like a good career move for me. Can I trust this guy to keep his hands off of me? He hasn't attempted anything while I paraded around in this skimpy thong bathing suit. He was recommended by a few of my friends. They would have told me if he made a move on them, wouldn't they? Is it really necessary to have nudes in my portfolio? My girlfriends never mentioned it but maybe they just assumed I would know.*

"Mark, have most of the women you photographed had the nudes taken?" Candie asked with attitude, trying to take the upper hand.

"I've photographed hundreds of women over the past five years, and to be honest I really don't know," Mark replied. He could tell she wasn't in love with his answer. He quickly added, "But if I had to guess about eighty percent routinely took off their tops during the session and maybe half of them took off the bottom, too. Some of them I convinced to do it, but most of them knew they had to have some nudes in their portfolios. Look, Candie, it's getting late, and I have a date in a few hours, so what do you want to do? We're all set up, so let's take the pictures and call it a day. Otherwise, if you decide to do this at some later date, I'll have to charge you another seven hundred dollars."

"I really can't afford that. All right, but let's ease into it. I really wasn't expecting to do nudes," her voice quivering slightly.

"Would you like a glass of wine? Maybe it will help you to relax a little."

"Yeah, I'll take the whole damn bottle," Candie joked.

Mark poured two glasses of the Cabernet Sauvignon he always had available for these occasions. *That was easier than I thought. I'll make her like me and the rest should be easy.*

"Now tell me the truth, exactly what kind of poses are these going to be, artistic or pornographic?" Candie asked while she took a big sip.

"Artistic and very sexy, but not pornographic. The producers and directors don't want to see porn. Have I said or done anything today that would make you think otherwise?" Mark quickly responded as he refilled the lead crystal goblets.

Candie downed the second glass of wine in one gulp, and stood up. With her back to Mark she removed her bikini top from under her chic satin robe and dropped both at her feet. "Okay, let's start with topless shots, and I'll see how it goes from there."

CHAPTER 5

Monday 5:00 PM

Doctor Darren Crowe, the newest member of the Medical Examiner's Office, slowly pulled the dildo out of the rectum of Alana Andrews, being careful not to rip any of the skin or tissue in the process. After careful examination of both the anus and the ten-inch dildo he concluded that some lubricate was used prior to insertion. Judging by the bruising around the anus and torn tissue in the rectum, it appeared that the dildo was pushed all the way in with one slow steady thrust and left there undisturbed until now. He decided it wasn't thrust in and out based on the way the tissue was torn in only one direction. He proceeded to take fluid and skin samples from both her rectum and vagina for his own preliminary testing and to send to the Connecticut Forensic Laboratory.

He decided to concentrate on the breasts next, removing both of the nipple piercings. Examining them under the microscope revealed that the word "bitch" was etched once into each piece of jewelry and that they were stamped 14-karat gold. The etching appeared to be crude and inconsistent, amateurish in nature. The breasts themselves were obviously augmented and enhanced, perfectly shaped and sized, pointing straight up in defiance of gravity. About a 40 D, he thought as he lost his professional attitude for a minute, allowing himself to think of what it would be like to sleep with a woman like Alana Andrews.

Doctor Crowe pulled each breast upward by the nipple towards her chin. Only a small faint scar tucked away under each breast revealed the surgical evidence of the procedure. *A beautiful job. Probably the work of Doctor Clemens.* He sliced open each breast and removed the implants, looking for the serial number and doctor's code number now required by most states.

"What'd you find out so far, Doc? Any fingerprints?" Frank asked as he and Brenda barged into the examination room located in the basement of the police station.

"Good evening, Detective Corrino," responded Doctor Crowe, ignoring Frank while he placed an implant under the microscope, while continuing to look for the numbers.

"Hi, there, Doctor Crowe," Brenda managed to respond with a flirty smile. "How's it going?"

"Did you find any fingerprints on the body or the dildos?" Frank asked again with some respect and a friendlier tone.

"Nope," Doctor Crowe replied as he looked up from the microscope to address the question. "As you can see I've only removed one so far. The body appears to have been scrubbed clean except for the blood on her upper thigh that probably oozed out during the transportation of the body. The makeup appears to have been applied within the last forty-eight hours."

"Was she raped in the traditional way?" Brenda inquired with little emotion.

"Yes, she was raped, and it looks like he left his semen inside intentionally. In fact a lot of semen, more than an average man would produce in one orgasm."

"Sodomized?"

"I don't think so."

"Are you suggesting that she was raped repeatedly or maybe gang raped?" Brenda asked.

"Yeah, maybe, one or the other. There's plenty of bruising on her inner thighs and vagina area. I'll know more later this evening when I get the preliminary lab results."

"Are you sure about that, Doc?" Frank asked.

"I'm not positive that all the fluid was semen. My preliminary lab test concluded that semen was present in the vagina."

"Why the hell would he take the time to wash away his fingerprints and yet leave his semen? Is it possible that he doesn't have a clue about how much DNA testing has evolved? How long before the full testing of the semen is completed?"

"It takes about seventy-two hours to get the conclusive results back from the state, Detective Gianni."

Doctor Crowe glanced over to Brenda, their eyes locking for a brief moment. "I should have my preliminary lab results in a few hours, Detective. Why don't you stop back, and we could go over the report. Maybe you could buy me dinner."

"Now that's a switch," Brenda replied, as she couldn't resist glancing over at Frank and winking. "I'll pick you up about eight, Doc. Will that give you enough time to clean up?"

"Why, you don't like my blood-stained jacket?" the doctor snapped back with a smirk.

Brenda was excited. She just wasn't sure if it was the prospect of having dinner with the young handsome doctor or getting the early results. A win-win situation, she concluded.

"What can you give us right now to help us think through this investigation?" Frank barged back into the conversation ignoring what had just taken place.

"You can sign out one of the nipple jewelry and check around with some of the street vendors to see if they recognize this beautiful piece of work. But I think you'll find that even they will say an amateur etched it. The murderer probably did it himself with a cheap, over-the-counter etching tool. Then you may want to pay Doctor Clemens a visit. He was probably the doctor who gave Ms. Andrews the perfect bust line. He's located in New York City, but I think he shares an office with a group in Greenwich. Other than what we discussed earlier, that's all I've got right now, Detective. You're welcome to hang around while I clear her throat and check for more semen."

"Let's go," Brenda told Frank as she headed out the door to avoid watching the removal of the phallic device. "I'll see you later, Doctor Crowe."

"Please, call me Darren," he shouted as he watched them disappear into the hallway.

"What's the matter with you?" Frank asked her when they got outside. "One of us should stay here and see what else he finds."

"I'm not going to watch him pull that damn thing out of her mouth. Maybe it turns you on, but it disgusts me. You can stay if you want, Frank, but he'll be telling me everything later anyway, and he can probably do a better job without us looking over his shoulder. Why don't you take his advice and follow up with the doctor and street vendors."

"What's gotten into you? Of course it wouldn't turn me on. I know that girl suffered a horrible death. What are you going to do?"

"I've got a date to get ready for, so I'm going to stop home and freshen up. You never know, Frank, I might get lucky!"

CHAPTER 6

Monday 8:00 PM

"Well, Doc, you clean up just fine," Brenda remarked when she returned to pick him up, trying not to overstate her joy of going out to dinner with him.

"Thank you, Detective. I must say you look lovely. I didn't think you were going to change your clothes. What a pleasant surprise, and please call me Darren. Do you mind if I call you Brenda?"

"I've been called worse," Brenda flirted back, "but you can save that for after dinner."

They both shared a laugh. *He is cute! Good thinking on my part to shower and change into something feminine. Maybe I'll get more than dinner from this guy after all.*

She wasn't sure what to wear for this meeting/date. So she decided on a flirty dress showing a touch of cleavage and some serious leg. She luxuriated in the sexy,look, trying to look like anything but a cop. She even wore a pair of FM's.

"So where shall we go?" Brenda asked.

"Since you're buying, I'll leave it up to you."

"Well, if that's the case, I guess the Burger Barn will do us just fine," she snapped back without missing a beat, while pushing open the door. "Don't forget the report, Doc. I intend to get something worthwhile for my money."

"Remember, Brenda, you get what you pay for!"

Brenda drove down to the Southport Brewery, a popular spot for decent food and a great selection of beer from the microbrewery on the premises. They had a few tables in a back corner that would provide them with some privacy.

"Hey, Detective," shouted the bartender as he caught a glimpse of her entering the restaurant. "Looking good!"

So much for trying to not look like a cop. "Hi, Gary, how you doing?" Brenda acknowledged. "I need one of those tables in the back corner," Brenda told the hostess.

"Sure, no problem," the hostess said as she led them to a table.

"Thanks, Hon, I really appreciate it."

"I guess you've never been here before?"

"Maybe once," Brenda laughingly replied. "So what have you got for me, Darren? Anything new in that report, or was this just an excuse to get a free meal?"

"Now that would be clever but highly unethical. I do have some more information. Do you have any leads on the murderer?"

"Nothing yet. It'll take three or four days to piece this thing together and come up with a list of suspects. So what do you have for me?"

Before he could answer, a waitress appeared to take their order. "Can I start you out with something to drink?"

"Sure. I'll have Blackstone Stout."

"And you, Miss?"

"I'll have a Razzbeery Blonde."

"Okay. I'll take your food order when I bring the beer."

"What are you smiling about?" Brenda asked Darren. "You're smirking from ear to ear."

"I thought you might order a Razzbeery Blonde, and I was right."

"Why did you think that?"

"Because you're a woman."

"Considering you're a doctor, it took you long enough to notice and not to mention you spent the day with a nude woman."

"Here you go," said the waitress as she placed the beers on the table. "Are you ready to order?"

"Bring us an order of Calamari, and I'll have the Crab Cakes."

"And you sir?"

"I'll have the Chicken Venezia."

"Do you want me to hold the entrees or do you want them served with the calamari?"

"Hold them."

They agreed to enjoy their dinner without discussing the case. After dinner they found it difficult to discuss the case in the crowded restaurant, and Brenda suggested they go back to her place on the beach so they could keep their discussion private.

"You have a place on the beach?"

"Yeah, I lease this small converted beach cottage on Fairfield Beach Road from a local businessman. He gave me a great deal because I'm a cop. He's got a summer cottage right next door to me, and he asked me to keep an eye on it when I'm home. He only uses it on the weekends although his daughter shows up occasionally during the week with a few girlfriends to catch some rays. The best thing about the house is the second floor where my bedroom resides. The room is complete with a mini-bar and small hot tub. I have a large slider that faces the ocean, too. Plus, I have a deck that I love to hang out on a warm night and listen to the ocean."

"Wow! I'm not going to ask you about your lease but I am curious about that hot tub. How many people can fit into a small hot tub? Is it like a personal unit for one?"

"Now what fun would it be if I couldn't soak with a few friends? Let's get going, okay? I've got to be in at eight tomorrow."

CHAPTER 7

Tuesday 8:30 AM

Frank anxiously waited for Brenda at her desk. The medical examiner apparently hadn't arrived yet either, according to the clerk on duty. Brenda and Frank were alike in many ways, although neither of them would ever admit it. No personal items adorned her desk. It was messy yet organized, just like his. He was tempted to pull open a few drawers, but lucky for him he hesitated just as Brenda walked in.

"Hi, Frank. What are you doing at my desk? Is everything all right?"

"Nothing, just waiting for you. So what info did you get out of the M.E. about Miss Andrews?"

"Gee, Frank, I just walked in. Let me grab a cup of coffee first."

Frank watched her as she walked over to the break room with a nice, natural wiggle. Something was different. She seemed to have an extra bounce in her step. She sort of had a little smirk on her face as she walked back.

"Okay, I give up. What's with the happy face? Win the lottery or something?"

"I don't know. I guess I slept well last night," Brenda managed to say with a much wider grin than before.

"All right, you have your damn coffee, so tell me what you learned last night."

"He said it appeared that Alana Andrews was gang-raped by at least three men. His preliminary testing resulted in finding three different DNAs mixed within the semen. Her anus was lubricated with some sort of oil, maybe massage oil, and the dildo was shoved in hard and fast, ripping some skin in the process. Based on the blood he found, he believes she was still alive at the time of penetration. The dildo being forced down her throat was the cause of death. But this time the killer toyed with her, putting it in and out, a little further down each time until she gagged. Then he would pull it out and let her catch her breath and then start again. It was pure torture until he decided to leave it stuck in her throat and watch her choke to death."

"Those sick bastards. Why? What did she do to deserve such a horrible death?"

"Wait, there's more. He found traces of Rohypnol in her blood."

"The date rape drug?"

"Yeah. He found bruising on her face that could have been made by some sort of mask, too. Also, marks on her ankles and wrists indicated that restraints were used."

"Wow, you got plenty. Anything else?"

"Only that the nipple piercing was the first thing done, and he can't be sure if the killer did the piercing or if she had them done just prior to her abduction."

"I talked to her roommates. They said she didn't sport nipple jewelry."

"Did they have any idea who could have hated her so much?"

Frank was deep in thought and ignored Brenda's question. "I wonder about the mask. If they planned to kill her from the start, it wouldn't matter if she saw their faces. See if he can get us more information about the mask. Maybe he could buy a few to figure out what this mask might have looked like, or at least what it covered."

"What difference does it make?"

"I don't know. Maybe nothing."

"Maybe it was some kind of a gang or college fraternity initiation that went wrong?"

"That's a possibility, but why not just tease her with the dildos? That would fit a sorority initiation ritual unless something went wrong and they accidentally killed her. Maybe they thought they could shift the blame to a gang. A gangbang, torture, and murder might fit gang revenge or a gang initiation. But they wouldn't go through the time to wash her, fix her hair, and pose her against a fucking tree. They would just dump her on the side of the road or in a ditch. Whoever did this was making a statement."

"So what else did you find out, Frank?"

"I started to tell you, I followed up on her address that the guys were able to dig up. Turns out she shared a house in Greenfield Hill with two other actress-model wannabes. I was able to speak with one of them. She was very upset, of course, when I told her what had happened. She said Miss Andrews had gone to the city three days ago to meet up with some friends from her Soap Opera days. She had just returned from a movie set in Texas and was looking forward to a little rest and relaxation with her friends. However, she never showed up in New York. Her friends called two days ago wondering why she didn't make the trip."

"The only trip she made was to Lake Mohegan."

"I also talked to McMillan about the crime scene. He said they did come up with something unusual at the crime scene. The ground at the body was wetter than the surrounding area. He sent several soil and foliage samples to the lab for analysis."

"Did the guys get us a name and address for Alana Andrews' agent?"

"Yeah, his name is Jay Martin. He also lives up in Greenfield Hill. Why are all these hot shots fleeing New York and invading Fairfield? Have you heard of him?"

"Yeah, he's been around the block a few times. He used to represent some of the bigger names but has recently turned his attention to young new talents. He was married to Cindee Cox. She got her start with Soap Operas, too."

"Why the divorce?"

"Rumor has it that she was cheating on him with the bodyguard that he hired to protect her. He was a retired police detective from the Los Angeles Police Department, the Hollywood Detective Division. I read all about it in the tabloids. I think his name was Perceo. Yeah, Tony Perceo."

"Why don't we pay this agent a visit and see what we can learn about Alana Andrews and Tony Perceo. After that, we can visit with her roommates again. Maybe you can bond with them and pick up on some of that female stuff," Frank added, trying to keep a straight face.

"Fuck you, Frank!"

CHAPTER 8

Tuesday 10:30 AM

The Greenfield Hill section of Fairfield was known for its grandiose beautiful homes, both old and new money, and for the Dogwood Festival held each May. The area was so different from the Lake Mohegan area, like night and day. The beautiful homes built by merchants and prosperous farmers during the late eighteenth century still remained. You could smell the money as you drove through Greenfield Hill. South of the green stood the Bronson Windmill, erected in the late nineteenth century to provide water for the Bronson estate. The Bronsons were credited with initiating the massive plantings of dogwood trees that still line the roads of the Greenfield Hill area today.

Heading north on Bronson Road approaching the Green, it was obvious that the house color of choice was white, the same color of the Greenfield Hill Congregational Church. Perhaps the

Historical Society insisted on white to keep everything in perspective.

"Take a right at the end of Bronson Road," Brenda said.

"Why not a left?"

"Because it's a right. I know how the house numbers run here. Take it slow, because you know the roads you're driving by are really driveways. Looks like that may be the driveway, Frank," Brenda said as they drove by it. "I think I saw the address carved in a stone pillar."

Frank backed up to the driveway and looked to see the house number for himself. "Yeah, I guess that's it, 667. You're right. If it wasn't for the number you could easily mistake this driveway for a road. Can't even see the house from here, can you?"

"I guess it's somewhere up the hill."

Frank proceeded to drive up the tree-lined driveway. Every twenty feet or so a dogwood tree stood at attention with it's buds at the earliest stage.

"This driveway must be a half mile long. Talk about your privacy. You could murder somebody up here and nobody would see anything."

"You could run a nudist colony up here and no one would know about it."

"And I hate when I see the guest homes on these properties. They're usually bigger and worth more than my house."

"Let's face it, Frank, these trees are worth more than our homes."

Suddenly before them stood a huge granite mansion, its beautiful reddish slate roof and black trim demanding their respect. Frank parked in the semi-circular driveway alongside a canary-yellow Hummer that dwarfed their unmarked police car. A newer, black Jaguar S-Type and silver Audi roadster were also parked further down. The topography was extensive and well established but not entirely kept. You would need a full-time caretaker to keep up with the landscaping, and apparently Mr. Martin didn't have one.

"Isn't it depressing, Brenda? You could work your ass off for a hundred years and never afford cars like these. That Jag eats ordinary cars like ours for lunch. Those three cars together are worth about two hundred grand."

As they approached the front door a woman could be heard screaming and crying. "Shut that fucking thing off, God damn it! You better call the police. Is this some kind of sick joke?"

Brenda rang the doorbell alongside the huge, oak double doors more than once before a door opened. The beautiful melody of the chimes continued to pour out the door as a frenetic Jay Martin appeared before them.

"You aren't those Jehovah Witnesses are you? Because if you are and you don't leave immediately, I'm calling the police. I'm tired of you people ignoring the no trespassing signs and showing up at my door preaching the Bible. So why don't you get the hell out of here and get a job!"

"Are you Jay Martin?" Frank asked as he flashed his I.D.

"Oh. You are the police. Sorry. What can I do for you, Detectives?"

"Do you know Alana Andrews?"

"I'm her agent. Or I guess was her agent. I was just going to call you guys."

"Why?"

"Let's take this inside okay. I've got something to show you."

They followed him through the large, marbled foyer and into a huge room filled with many sofas, chairs, and cocktail tables. Taller cocktail tables for use while standing were scattered throughout the room as well. One wall was completely mirrored, making the room appear twice as large, and a beautiful mahogany bar took up a corner. A huge plasma television was mounted on the wall with a still image of Alana Andrews, lying on a bed, totally naked except for a dildo deep down her throat.

The detectives were momentarily shocked and speechless as Jay Martin walked over to a DVD player and ejected the disc, causing the television screen to go blank.

"Where did you get that, Mr. Martin?" Frank asked as Martin handed him the DVD.

"Please call me Jay, Detective," he replied as he picked up the DVD case and an envelope that the DVD apparently arrived in and handed them over to Brenda. "I found it in my mailbox. I assumed it was a solicitation for representation. I get these things sent to me all the time."

"You said you found it in your mailbox?" Brenda inquired.

"Yeah, that's right."

"The envelope has no address or postage. How do you suppose it ended up in your mailbox?"

"I guess somebody put it in there. What? Do you think it just magically appeared in my mailbox? Look, people find out my address and just drive by and stick these things in the fucking mailbox. Look I'll show you a few that I received and kept as possibilities," he said as he walked over to a wooden case with glass doors filled with CDs, DVDs, and videotapes. He returned with a few of each to make his point.

"How often do you find these things in your mailbox?" Frank asked.

"Two or three times a month I guess."

"Was anyone with you when you found this one?"

"I was," a voice answered from a settee. She slowly sat up and made herself visible to everyone. "I was the one that took that disgusting DVD from the mailbox."

"And you are?" Brenda asked as she walked towards the woman.

"Margo…Margo Delaney. Hey, why are you writing my name in your book?"

"Why does it concern you, Ms. Delaney? Do you have something to hide?"

"No! I hope you don't think I had anything to do with that DVD."

"Did you know Alana Andrews?"

"Yeah, I know her. Knew her. I met her here at a party."

"When did you see her last?"

"Around Christmas time."

"Where was that?"

"Here. Jay had a party."

"Would you like to see the DVD from the beginning?" asked Martin. "You can watch it on my big screen. It's very graphic. At first I thought it was a scene from a movie script or something. But knowing that she was dead, I realized the bastard who killed her must have made the recording."

"How did you find out she was murdered?" Brenda asked. "The story hasn't been on the news yet."

"I've got connections."

"Why give it to you?" Frank asked. "Is somebody out to ruin you?"

"I don't know. Killing one of my clients isn't going to ruin me. I have many clients that are doing quite well and keeping me in this lifestyle. I also have similar homes in Hawaii and California for the winter months."

"Then what were you doing here last Christmas?"

"I had a party. I flew a few friends back with me from California, and the other guests like Alana lived here in Fairfield. She shares a house with two women about a mile from here. Would you like me to look up the address?"

"No. That won't be necessary. Do you plan to be in town for

a while? We may need to ask you a few more questions."

Turning his attention to Brenda he stated, "I'm having a party this weekend. Why don't you stop by and meet some of my friends? Many of them knew Alana."

"Do you really think her friends will feel like partying?"

"Maybe not her real friends."

Frank got into his face. "Why don't you do the right thing and cancel the party in her honor?"

Jay didn't answer. Brenda looked over at Margo without actually asking her if she was going to the party, Margo just sank back down into the settee to avoid having to answer. *These fucking people are unbelievable!*

"Frank let's get out of here. The stench is making me sick."

As they both headed for the door Frank told Jay Martin to write down his home and cell phone numbers in his notebook.

"What can you tell us about Tony Perceo?"

"He's the son of a bitch that broke up my marriage. I hired him to protect my wife. Instead I catch him making out with her in my own house. So I fired his ass and got a divorce. End of story."

"Weren't you married to Cindee Cox?" Brenda asked.

"Yeah, that's right."

"So did she and Tony Perceo continue their relationship?"

"I have no idea, Detective. Trust me when I say I don't give two shits about either one of them. Besides, what's that got to do with anything?"

"Did you know he was Alana Andrews's bodyguard?"

"No. You think he has something to do with this?"

"Probably not," Frank interrupted.

Once outside Frank turned back towards the house and shouted to Jay, "Which car is yours?"

"I own the Hummer and the Jag. Why?"

"Just curious. Two people and three cars."

Brenda was already in the car when Frank finally opened the door. "Did you get all the plate numbers?"

"Of course."

"Jay, why didn't you tell him who owned the Audi?" asked Ms. Delaney.

"Fuck him. He didn't ask, did he?"

CHAPTER 9

Tuesday 12:00 PM

The home that Alana Andrews once occupied wasn't very far from Jay Martin's house, only about a half-mile or so down from Old Academy Road. An impressive home in its own right, but nothing like the mansion of Jay Martin. No long driveway or impressive landscaping for this house, but the large white wooden colonial with black shutters had plenty of character. It was built fifty years ago when a colonial was a colonial. It's located at the end of a cul-de-sac that offered the rear of the house plenty of privacy. Frank wanted Brenda to interview the two women because he thought they might open up to her.

The afternoon was fairly warm for April, with plenty of sunshine poking through the trees. That was one thing about Greenfield Hill, the roads and properties are abounding with large tall trees, except for the dogwoods. They are much smaller in comparison but plentiful.

Frank rang the doorbell of the front door. His eyes were drawn to the original bird and tree carvings that were etched into the raised panels of the red door. He pressed the doorbell again, this time straining to hear if it was working.

"Try knocking, Frank. Maybe they can't hear the bell," Brenda said, trying to calm down his growing impatience.

Just as he started to knock the door swung open. An attractive young women wrapped in a towel appeared before them.

"Detective, you're back?" the attractive brunette inquired as she pulled the towel a little tighter.

"Yes. I'm sorry we pulled you out of the shower. My partner and I have a few more questions for you and your housemate. Is she available?"

"I wasn't in the shower. I was trying to catch a few rays and I was listening to music with my headphones. I faintly heard the doorbell chimes, so I pulled them off to listen. I heard the chimes clearly the second time."

"You can hear the door bell from the backyard?"

"No silly. I wasn't outside. There's a room at the back of the house that's made mostly with glass, even the roof. Like a solarium. Come in, and I'll show you what I mean."

They followed her towards the back of the house, noting that the house was nicely furnished with antiques and that the rooms were large and airy. She led them into a small, narrow room that was extremely bright and warm but scantly furnished. The first four feet of the walls were wainscoting and the rest was made with glass blocks. The ceiling was entirely made of glass as well. Three beach-style lounge chairs rested in the middle of the small room. A lime-green wooden piece of furniture with two drawers topped with a variety of suntan lotions, and two dirty martini glasses separated two of the chairs. The floor was covered with a rug that resembled beach sand.

"Wow. This is so cute. I'm Detective Corrino by the way. What's your name?"

"Janet. Janet Mays."

They briefly shook hands while Frank took out his notebook to take notes.

"This room is so cool. Are you able to use it all year round?"

"Pretty much. It doesn't have heat so when it's bitter cold outside it doesn't get warm enough in here to be enjoyable for sun tanning. But sometimes we'll bring in a portable space heater to keep it warm. It's like our escape-from-reality room."

"Janet, did Alana like to tan in here, too?"

"Sure, we all did. We'd pretend we were on a tropical island with a bunch of hot guys all around, bringing us our drinks, and rubbing us up with sun tan lotion." Janet looked over at Frank, realizing she momentarily forgot he was there and immediately began to blush.

"Detective Gianni told me that you are positive that Alana didn't have her nipples pierced, is that correct?"

"Yes, I'm sure of it"

"And how can you be so sure?"

With her back to Frank, Janet opened her towel to Brenda revealing her tanned nude body with no tan lines. "We always tan in the nude. We had one of our tanning parties the night before she left, and believe me, her nipples were not pierced."

"Did these tanning parties involve more than tanning?"

"What do you mean?"

"Did you girls, like, touch each other? Do anything sexual to each other?"

"Well, we did take turns rubbing each other with suntan lotion. Sometimes it was quite sensual, especially after a few drinks. But after that you were on your own. We aren't lesbians, if that's what you mean. If someone had a need they would use a vibrator on themselves and we would pretend not to notice. We didn't touch each other except for when we applied the suntan lotion. I guess it did turn into a contest of sorts, you know, turning each other on with a full body massage and trying to get each other hot enough to resort to the vibrator. But it was out of love. We work real hard all week to survive and also go to auditions at the drop of a hat. With a ninety percent turn-down rate, you need something to look forward to."

"Would you mind showing me the vibrators?"

Janet looked towards Frank and then back to Brenda.

"Frank, would you excuse us for a minute?" Brenda asked.

"No problem," he said as he left the solarium.

Janet opened the two green drawers to reveal about six vibrators, each a different size, style, and color. But they were toys compared to the two weapons that violated Alana Andrews.

"Are there any missing?"

"No, I don't think so."

"Did any of you have others that maybe you kept in your bedrooms?"

"I don't. I don't know if Alana or Sarah have any. They never mentioned it. I really don't think they did. We were pretty close and didn't keep secrets from each other. If anything, if one of them had a new vibrator she would have been willing to let us try it. Why don't we check her room?"

"That was my next question. Have you or Sarah gone into her room while she's been gone?"

"No. We don't have many house rules, but that was one of them. You don't go into someone's room without permission. Everyone needs to have her own private space."

They joined Frank in the living room where he was snooping around, looking at some photographs.

"Come on, Frank, we're going to check out Alana's bedroom."

"Yeah, okay. Who are some of the people in these pictures?"

"Oh, just a few friends."

"When you have a chance could you make me a list of everyone in these pictures along with their phone numbers?"

"I doubt if I have most of their phone numbers, but I'll give you what I can."

All three bedrooms were located on the second floor. Alana's room was the furthest down the hallway. A simple colonial fixture attached to the wall next to the bathroom provided the hall light. The room's décor wasn't at all what the detectives expected. Pastel pink and purple flowers decorated the bedspread of a queen-sized bed that fit perfectly between two windows. Two large French provincial bureaus stood at attention on two other walls, beckoning for someone to open its drawers. A large, full-length mirror adorned the far wall. Next to it hung a large poster of Alana Andrews in a skimpy outfit that was promoting her new movie.

"Doesn't she look beautiful?" asked Janet.

Frank pulled open one of the beckoning bureau drawers, pulled out some things, and examined them. He noticed a small jewelry box in the drawer and started to handle some of the pieces.

"Detective Gianni. Please stop. Please don't handle her things. What are you looking for?"

"Anything and everything. I'm rather surprised by the modest furnishings and cheap jewelry of someone who was making a few million dollars for that picture," pointing to the poster.

"She was just starting to make it. She still owes a lot of money. She was planning to buy a house next year if things worked out."

"Maybe I can stop by and look around in a day or two after you've had a chance to rest."

"I'll tell you what, Detective. I'll go through everything tomorrow and pull out any photographs and jewelry that I find and put them in a box for you. I don't feel comfortable with you handling her stuff here in her room."

"Sure. That will be fine, Janet. Also look around for the item that we discussed downstairs, too. If you find one it could be important to the case."

Brenda interjected. "Janet, I'm sorry but I have to ask. Why aren't you more upset about Alana's murder?"

"Upset? I'm too terrified to be upset. In fact, Sarah and I are thinking of calling Alana's former bodyguard to ask him to keep an eye on us for a while. He used to be a cop in California."

"Did you say he was her former bodyguard?" Frank asked.

"Yeah. She hired him about three months ago to keep an eye on her because she thought she was being stalked by someone. He never saw anyone following her, and she decided that whoever it was had stopped, so about two weeks ago she decided she didn't need him anymore. I guess that was a big mistake."

Tears began to roll down Janet's face.

Finally some emotion.

"I probably got her killed. I used to make fun about her having a bodyguard and told her I was going to invite him to one of our tanning parties so he could keep a really close eye on her while she tanned herself. Maybe she would have kept him on if I'd kept my big mouth shut."

Brenda embraced her as she cried, noticing a faint smell of tanning lotion from her neck.

"Was the bodyguard Tony Perceo?" Brenda spoke softly into Janet's hair.

"Yeah, do you know him? He was also Cindee Cox's bodyguard for a while, too. That's how Alana got to know him. Cindee helped her get a few bit parts in the beginning of her career. She lived right up the street from here with her husband Jay Martin. He's an agent. They're divorced now. Jay thought Tony instigated an affair with her but it wasn't true. Cindee wanted Tony, but he refused to give in to her. He told her that he was hired to protect her, and that was all he planned on doing. But she continued to put the moves on him every chance she got. She even let him see her naked a few times, accidentally on purpose. Some of my friends say she's a nymphomaniac, and she likes women, too. Jay walked in on her one day, and she had her arms wrapped around Tony. He went ballistic and told both of them to get out of his house and to never come back. Tony tried to explain, but Jay wouldn't listen."

"What about Alana? Was she serious with anyone?"

"No."

"Do you know where Cindee lives now?"

"She rents a small house in Southport on Oldfield Road. I don't know the address. When Sarah gets home I can find out. Do you need it? I can call you when I get it."

"Yeah, that would be helpful," she said as she handed her business card to her. "Doesn't Sarah have a cell phone?"

"Yeah but she keeps it off while she's working."

"What's she doing, a play or something?"

"She dances at the Paradise Club in Stamford."

"She's a stripper?"

"An exotic dancer. She has to dance topless, but it's up on a stage that's a good ten feet from the nearest patron. It's a very professional gig, and it pays twenty dollars an hour plus tips."

"Did Alana ever work there?"

"No."

"What about you?"

"No. I've been able to get by just fine with my acting jobs.

Sarah hasn't been as lucky, so on the weekends she works at the club and fills in once in a while during the week."

"Where does Tony Perceo live?"

"He lives at Pine Creek Condominiums at the end of Pine Creek Road, but I don't know which unit. Please catch the bastards that killed Alana before they kill again. Is it true that she was gang-raped and tortured?"

"Where did you hear that?"

"On the radio."

"I wouldn't believe everything you hear on the news."

Frank couldn't help but ask, "Why do you think they will kill again?"

"I don't know. I guess because they always do, don't they?"

They didn't answer her as they headed towards the front door. Once outside, Brenda turned to Janet and gave her another hug.

"Give me a call if you need to talk or think of anything else about Alana that might help us out okay?"

"Thanks," she said as she managed to show a brave face.

"What the fuck do they expect?" Frank said when they got inside the car. "Laying around in a glass room bare-ass and playing with vibrators. Probably playing with each other, too. No wonder they're being stalked."

"That's what I like about you, Frank. You're not afraid to speak your mind no matter how stupid it makes you look."

"Yeah, well, try parading around naked on your deck some night, and let me know if you attract any attention."

"Fuck you, Frank."

"That's what I thought. Should we head down to Pine Creek Condominiums and look up Tony Perceo?"

"I guess so," Brenda answered. "I'm surprised it made the news already. So much for trying to keep it quiet for a while."

CHAPTER 10

Tuesday 3:30 PM

Within Fairfield like every other town or city, you had the good, the bad, and the ugly, although one could easily argue that the ugly side of Fairfield was much nicer than some of the so-called good areas of many of the surrounding towns and cities.

Driving from Greenfield Hill over to Pine Creek Road was like going from night to day. Yet on its own merit, the area was very nice. Pine Creek Road intersected with the Post Road a mile or so up from the police station area. Many of the homes were smaller here than the guest homes of the mansions of Greenfield Hill, maybe even smaller than some of their garages.

The Pine Creek Condominiums were built back in the mid nineteen-eighties during the residential building boom. Housing developments were popping up everywhere in Fairfield County like weeds. Pine Creek Road ended at the beach and that's where the condominiums were located. A recent coat of beige paint suited the building well, soothing the weather beaten concrete for one's eyes. Being right on the beach with each unit having a balcony was obviously the main attraction. The Beachside Bar and Grill was within walking distance, known for its quiet days and rowdy nights, attracting the college crowd from nearby Fairfield University to party on the weekends. If it weren't for the location, these condos would be a hard sell in Fairfield by today's upscale housing standards. Yet today, the units could easily command $350,000 for a 1000-square-foot, two-bedroom home.

The time was four o'clock in the afternoon, and the condominium association watchdog for the day was sitting in the office when Frank and Brenda arrived. The woman appeared to be a well-preserved seventy something. She was too busy reading an *Enquirer* to look at the detectives as they walked into the tiny closet of an office.

"Does Tony Perceo live here?" Frank asked.

"Who wants to know?" she replied without lifting her head.

"The Fairfield Police Department," Frank replied as they both pulled out their badges and got her attention.

"What's he done?"

"We just want to talk to him. Does he live here or not?" Brenda said as she put her hand over Brad Pitt's face.

"He's in 2-C."

"Do you know if he's home?"

"I have no idea. Do you think we sit around all day and spy on each other?"

"No. But since you were sitting here I thought you might have seen him leave," Frank said harshly.

"Go out and check his parking spots. Every unit has two assigned parking spots, and they are marked with the unit number.

"Thanks," Brenda said sweetly, trying to win her over.

A white Porsche Boxster occupied the space marked 2-C."Looks like everybody has a better car than we do," Brenda remarked as she looked into the interior of the Porsche.

Unit 2-C was one of the end units on the second floor with the balcony facing the water. They listened at the door before pressing the doorbell button. Frank Sinatra was singing at a moderate volume. They could hear nothing else, just old blue eyes singing his heart out.

Brenda rang the doorbell but "The Lady is a Tramp" was louder, and no one came to open the door. So Frank knocked rather forcibly to insure that he would be heard over the sound of the music.

Within a few seconds the door swung open with vigor. "What can I do for you, Detectives?"

"Takes one to know one," replied Frank, regretting immediately that he revealed that he knew something about Perceo's background. *Damn it! A rookie mistake!*

"Are you Tony Perceo?" Frank asked.

"Yes."

"We'd like to ask you a few questions about Alana Andrews. Do you have a few minutes?"

"Sure, come on in. What a shame. She was on her way to stardom. She was going to be huge," he said as he lowered the volume on his surround sound system.

Tony Perceo was an impressive presence, over six feet tall with auburn hair, cobalt eyes, and a well-disciplined body. His home was equally striking, decorated with beautiful, oriental-style furniture and wall hangings. The unit was much nicer than one could imagine from the outside. A marble fireplace with a nice cozy fire emanated an inviting smell of cedar even though it was obviously a gas-burning ceramic log. Brenda couldn't stop herself from occasionally looking up at a very large photograph of a gorgeous nude woman that hung above the mantle.

"That's my wife," Tony volunteered. "Isn't she stunning?"

"Yes, very beautiful, and she looks very familiar. Is she here?" Brenda asked.

"She passed away a few years ago from cancer: breast cancer. She was only thirty-seven. She was an actress and a wonderful wife. She could leave her work at the studio. When she was home she was an everyday person like you and me. She gave me that photograph for my fortieth birthday seven years ago. She was thirty years old and in her prime."

"I'm so sorry. What was her stage name?"

"Janet Jennings."

"That's right. I remember her now. She did most of her work on the stage, didn't she?"

"She always said that performing on stage was the purest form of acting. Although she was considering a few movie offers shortly before she became ill. They were actually less demanding and paid better."

"Can I offer either of you a drink? Oh, forgive me. You are obviously on duty. Are you really a detective?" he asked Brenda, flirting openly. "They didn't have policewomen as pretty as you in New York."

Before Brenda could answer Frank asked, "Why did you retire so early?"

"So I could be there for my wife during her illness. We sold our home in New York and moved here. She wanted to spend her remaining days near the ocean."

"Why Fairfield, Connecticut?"

"The condo was very affordable, and she had a few friends living in the area."

"Did she know Alana Andrews?" Frank asked.

"No. I don't think so. I met her after Janet died. A friend of mine, Dave Williams, another retired cop, is a private investigator, and he introduced me to her. She was looking for someone to keep an eye out for her because she thought a fan was stalking her. Dave's a one-man operation and already had a gig, so he couldn't help her out. So he offered me the job to keep me busy and help me get over Janet. So I followed her around and staked out her house several times over a two-month period but there was no stalker. I think she was feeling anxious because her career was starting to take off, and people were starting to recognize her around town."

"Do you have a phone number and address for Mr. Williams?"

"Sure," Tony said as he walked over to his computer desk and picked up a business card. "You can keep it. I have plenty."

"What can you tell us about Jay Martin?"

"He's made a lot of money off the talent of many young women and has no appreciation for the hard work and dedication it takes for an actress to make it."

"He doesn't like you either," Brenda added with a flirty smile of her own. "He says you stole his wife from him."

"That's because he's an idiot. She was just trying to make him jealous because she was very upset with all the young wannabes that hung all over him everyday. Don't think for a minute that he wasn't sleeping with them. Those girls would do anything to get appointments to read for just a bit part."

"So you never had an affair with Cindee Cox?"

"No. I don't mess with married women. She called me a few times after he threw her out, but I didn't return her calls."

"Why did he hire you?"

"To keep an eye on Cindee while he spent time in New York and Hollywood, drumming up appointments for his clients."

"Did you sleep there during those times?"

"Yes."

"And you never slept with her?"

"No."

"What does this have to do with Alana Andrews?"

"I don't know. Maybe nothing," Frank answered.

"Where does Cindee Cox live now?"

"Right around the corner over on Oldfield Road, number 367 I think. I know what you're thinking, but I only know she lives there from what people have told me. I've never been in her house."

"Just one more question, then we'll leave you with old blue eyes and your wine. Do you hate all talent agents or just Jay Martin?"

"Let's just say I don't like people that use people for financial gain and show them no respect."

"Okay. We'll be in touch if we have any more questions."

"I'm very sorry about your wife. She was very talented and a true beauty," Brenda added.

"Thank you. I really appreciate you saying that."

*

When they got back to their car they decided to check out Cindee Cox's house since it was just around the corner. Just about all the homes on Oldfield Road were small capes. The entire street looked out of place in this neighborhood. They pulled into the driveway of 367 Oldfield Road. The simple white house appeared lifeless. No fancy cars in the driveway, just a red Honda Accord. No slate roof or fancy front door. Definitely not the house of a movie star.

They rang the doorbell and knocked on the front and rear doors but no one answered. Peering into the windows they saw a nicely furnished unoccupied home. They were about to leave when an elderly woman dressed in a burgundy jogging outfit approached them.

"Can I help you folks?" asked the elderly woman who appeared to be of Polish or Hungarian ancestry.

"Yes. I'm Detective Corrino, and this is Detective Gianni. We wanted to speak to Cindee Cox. Do you know where she is or when she'll be home?"

"I haven't seen her since yesterday morning. She said she was bicycling down to Sasco Beach."

"What's your name?"

"Mrs. Pucho."

"Do you live there?" Frank asked while pointing to the gray house next door.

"Yes. I've lived here for the past forty years. I lost my husband a few years ago to cancer. My daughter wants me to sell and move in with her. I like it here. Why should I move? How many people can say they have an actress living next door to them?"

"Does she bicycle to the beach often?"

"Once the weather starts to get nice she goes about three times a week. During the summer she'll even go at night once in a while."

"I didn't think she'd be home much, being an actress."

"Her work is sporadic. Sometimes she will be gone for a month and then be home for three months. I get her mail and feed her cat when she's away."

"Does she live alone?"

"Yes."

"How about any boyfriends?"

"I don't know about any steady boyfriends, but she has had a man stay overnight occasionally. I'm sure she could have a different man every night if she wanted. She's only in her twenties and very pretty. Oh, and those eyes. She has beautiful, emerald green eyes."

"How about girlfriends?"

"Not really."

"Any wild parties?"

"No."

"Have you ever seen a white Porsche, a yellow Hummer, a black Jaguar, or a silver Audi parked in her driveway?"

"Gee I don't know one car from another. I think I've seen white and silver cars here."

"Here's my card," said Brenda. Please give it to Miss Cox and ask her to call me."

"Okay. What's this all about anyway? Is she in some kind of trouble?"

"We just want to ask her a few questions about a friend of hers."

They headed back to the police station, and they checked their messages and questioned the other detectives working on the investigation. Nobody had anything significant to add. Tomorrow would be the third day since the body was discovered and they had no significant suspects or leads.

"Forensics will have copies of the DVD for us in the morning, and whatever else they've discovered. I'm surprised I haven't heard from Doctor Crowe again. I guess he hasn't received the detailed report from the lab yet. He probably decided to wait until he had something for me."

"You must be losing your touch, Brenda. I would think that the young doctor would have something to offer you every day."

"Very funny, Frank. Look at the bright side; I won't be late for work tomorrow."

"You take a look at the DVD in the morning. I'm going to stop by the Easton P.D. and talk to them about the rookie that discovered the body. I'll ask for permission to interview him. I don't want to step on anybody's toes. If he's on duty, all the better. You can fill me in on the DVD when I get back."

CHAPTER 11

Wednesday 8:00 AM

Brenda arrived at work at eight o'clock. After she grabbed a cup of coffee she began to go over what she and Frank had discovered so far. First there was Jay Martin, the rich talent scout. Alana's death would cost him money. He didn't appear to have any reason to kill her. Why did someone deliver the DVD to him? Then there's Tony Perceo the bodyguard. She dismissed him as her bodyguard two weeks before she was found dead. Perhaps she was killed to keep her mouth shut about something. Maybe the dildo in her throat was a metaphor. Maybe there was something going on between Tony and Cindee Cox. Perhaps Alana threatened to tell Jay Martin, and Tony killed her to shut her up. Cindee was already divorced from Jay, so what would it matter? Then again, he was hired because she thought she was being stalked. Maybe this stalker killed her as soon as she stopped having Tony watch her. Maybe Tony was the stalker! One thing for sure, there was too many damn maybes.

"Excuse me, Detective Corrino; I was told to bring you these two DVD copies and these preliminary forensic and toxicology reports."

"Thank you. And you are who?"

"Mike Francis. I work in the forensics lab part time as an intern. I'm a law student at Fairfield University. I'm sort of assigned to this Alana Andrews case. Well, actually, I asked if I could work on it. This is a fascinating murder case, don't you think?"

"Fascinating? Since when is a brutal rape and murder fascinating? Are you into humiliating woman or raping them?"

"I…I didn't mean anything by it," the fair-haired college boy stammered.

"Well, if you think that murder is fascinating…oh, just forget it."

"I'm sorry. I apologize. Fascinating was the wrong word to use. I just meant that it was intriguing, you know, different."

"Yeah, whatever," Brenda said calmly, realizing that she flew off the handle for no reason. "Have you seen Doctor Crowe today?"

"No."

"If you do, tell him to call me as soon as he receives the final report from the state lab."

"Sure. No problem. Again I apologize for my poor choice of words."

"Forget about it. I shouldn't have jumped down your throat."

The preliminary report held no surprises. The lab discovered two sets of fingerprints on the DVD. *Undoubtedly Jay Martin's and Margo Delaney's.* The DVD was produced by a Hitachi DVD Camcorder that records directly on to a DVD disc, instead of onto tape or digital media memory. The Hitachi DVD Camcorder was considered a high-end consumer product, with a retail value of two thousand dollars and up.

Brenda wandered over to the media room where they have two PCs, a combination VCR/DVD player, and a twenty-five-inch, flat-screen television, located in a large converted storage room. Unlike neighboring cities and towns, this equipment was state-of-the-art, donated by a local civic organization. She closed the door, put on the headphones, and popped the disc into the DVD drive. The television screen became alive as it portrayed a woman, stark naked, laying spread eagle on a beautiful antique mahogany bed, facing the ceiling. She was wearing a mask made with assorted colored feathers that extend down to about the middle of her chest. *Darren was right about the mask!* Her arms and legs were tied to the bedposts with rope. The rope appeared to be the same type that bound her to the tree. Another person enters into view, his back to the camcorder. The camcorder records as he proceeds to crudely pierce each nipple with a long thin straight needle. She winces from the pain.

"Ouch! That hurts. Why did you do that? Please let me go," she cries out. "I don't know who you are. I won't tell anyone. A very small amount of blood became visible as he forced the jewelry through the piercing of each nipple.

"That hurts," she said again while straining her neck to get a look at her stinging nipples. "Please stop. I haven't seen your face. Please let me go."

The screen goes black for about ten seconds and then it starts again. She appears to be alone. A man enters the room and kneels between her legs.

"Please help me," she says as she strains to lift her head and see what the man was doing. "I'm being held here against my will. Please call the police." His hand brushes along her thigh and rests on her pubic hair. "Please leave me alone," she pleads.

The man ignores her pleas as he fingers her vagina very slowly for at least a minute and then places his finger into his mouth, sucking on it with obvious pleasure. He then bends over to perform oral sex on her but changes his mind. By the look on his face he was about to lose control. He quickly undoes his pants, exposing his bony ass and his completely aroused penis. It's obvious that he penetrates her at this point. Unlike a porn movie, there aren't any close ups of the penetration, but it was obvious he was raping her.

"Get off of me. Leave me alone," she yelled as she thrusts her pelvis up to try to throw him off her. "Stop! I said stop," she screams as tears begin to run down both sides of her face from beneath the mask.

But he doesn't stop. He continues to rape her and quickly reaches his climax. Before he gets off of her he grabs her breasts, taking a close look at the piercings, flicking his tongue over each nipple, all the time keeping his back to the view finder. He withdraws from her and leaves the room, obviously shielding his face from the camcorder. She cries softly for about twenty seconds until rapist number two enters the room.

"What do you want? Leave me alone you son of a bitch! Do you know who I am? I'm Alana Andrews and I'm being held here against my will. Please leave here and call the police. I'll give you as much money as you want. Anything...anything you want!"

Again she was greeted with silence. She was raped again and this time the man took his time, unlike the first man who couldn't hold back his climax. This man appears to be actually enjoying every moment. When he reaches his orgasm he grunts rather loudly, proudly showing that he has reached his climax. Unlike the first man, he quietly leaves without touching her further. As soon as he leaves, another man enters the room and proceeds to rape her as well, her plea once again falling on deaf ears. This man holds onto her breasts for leverage as he rams away. He's by far the most aggressive, as he also ignores her pleas and continues to pound her. He takes the longest to finish the dirty deed as he ejaculates with a flourish of absolute joy. Before he leaves he grabs her left leg and twists it upward so that her ass cheeks are raised. He gives them a hard loud slap, causing her to scream and burst into an uncontrollable crying jag. *Thank you ma'am.* As he leaves he deliberately turns and faces the camcorder on his way out. He was wearing a Mickey Mouse mask!

The screen again goes black for about twenty seconds. The next scene begins with a person standing at the foot of the bed, rubbing a large glistening dildo between her breasts.

She can hardly talk while she's crying. "Please help me. I can give you money, a lot of money. Please untie me. Help me to escape. I haven't seen any of your faces. I can't tell anyone who you are."

Again her words are ignored as the person continues to rub and spin the dildo between and over her breasts, stopping to make circles around her nipples. *The shiny substance must be the massage oil that Darren said was present in her rectum.* He slowly drags the dildo down from her chin, between her breasts, over her belly, and down to her ass. He proceeds to slowly penetrate her rectum with the dildo as her soft muffled crying changes to a scream from the unbearable pain, as he shoves it quickly, all the way up to the balls. She appears to have passed out at this point. The figure leaves and once again the screen becomes black.

Barely audible crying could be heard when the recording began again. She was sobbing softly. The camcorder lens was zoomed in on her buttocks. The rubber testicles were staring out like giant frogeyes toward the camcorder as a small amount of blood trickling between her cheeks and on to the sheet. Brenda was using all her inner strength to force herself to continue to watch the recording knowing what was next. But she has to watch it. It's her job to watch it. The camcorder fanned over her body from toe to head and stopped on her face.

The figure once again entered the room, this time standing at the far side of the bed near her head and facing the camcorder. He was wearing the Mickey Mouse mask and showing her that he has another large dildo in his hand. The victim said something, barely audible, a whisper, perhaps another plea. The villain pulled off her mask, and there was no doubt that the victim was Alana Andrews. He placed the dildo into her mouth, gently pushing it in and out, as a flood of tears flow onto her neck and shoulders. He pushed it a little deeper with each stroke until she gagged. He left it in place and walked around to the other side of the bed, his back to the viewfinder now. He pulled off his mask and placed it on her stomach, wanting her to know who he was, now that he was going to kill her. You could see by her expression that she recognized him. She looked surprised. She tried to speak but couldn't. All you could see now was his motion of pushing and pulling the dildo in and out of her throat as she gagged with each thrust and gasped for air each time he pulled it out. Finally he pushed it in all the way and left the room, allowing the camcorder to record her slow death. As she choked to death the camcorder zoomed in on her face, forcing the viewer to witness the horrendous death up close, the dildo buried deep into her throat, right up to the balls. Once again the scene went black. *Thank God it's over.*

Brenda released many tears of her own, ruining her makeup and wetting her shirt. She quickly walked to the ladies room so that she could throw up. Once she regained her composure, she cleaned herself up, applied new makeup, and went back to her desk, avoiding any eye contact with the other detectives.

Brenda was still sick to her stomach. She felt like she was the one repeatedly abused and murdered. She couldn't think straight. She could only think of catching the bastards and castrating them. *I'll cut theirs off and shove it down their throats. Let's see how they like it!* She was contemplating booking out a few hours of sick time and going home to a gratifying soak in the hot tub to sooth away her disgust.

Just then the phone rang and it was Doctor Crowe to the rescue.

"I hear you're looking for me. What's up?"

"Do you have anything new on the Alana Andrews case?"

"No. The state lab results haven't come back yet. What's wrong? Are you okay?" he asked sensing something was wrong.

"Don't waste any time looking into the masks. They're on the DVD. Viewing the DVD got me upset."

"What DVD?"

"Oh, I thought you knew. We have a DVD of the rapes and murder. It appears to have been recorded by the murderous bastards themselves as the final character assassination of Alana Andrews."

"How did you get it?"

"The DVD was delivered to Alana Andrews' agent, Jay Martin. He lives up in Greenfield Hill."

"Wow! Maybe he's the killer. He could be trying to throw you off track."

"No. We don't have a motive. With her death he would lose money, now and in the future. Why haven't you called me? I guess you didn't enjoy yourself the other night."

"No. I mean yes. I had a great time. I've been busy, that's all. Maybe we could get together this weekend?"

"Can't. It's my weekend to work. How about tonight?"

"Tonight?"

"Yeah, tonight. What's wrong with tonight? You have to work or something?"

"No. You caught me by surprise, that's all. Tonight's good. I'll pick up some dinner and bring it to your house. How's seven-thirty sound?"

"Sounds like a cheap date."

If you'd rather go out, I guess we could do that."

"Hey. I'm just yanking your chain. That's the best offer I've had this week. Seven-thirty's perfect."

CHAPTER 12

Frank stopped by the Easton Police Department and found out that Patrolman Jason Miller was working. The dispatcher contacted him on the radio and told him that Frank would like to meet him at Sliverman's Farm on Sport Hill Road in ten minutes.

Patrolman Miller was standing outside his police car, parked at the far end of the parking lot, when Frank arrived. He was a young, good-looking guy, with a very athletic build. He stood about six feet tall. A typical rookie, Frank thought, except for having a full head of hair.

They shook hands as Frank introduced himself.

"Patrolman Miller? I'm Homicide Detective Frank Gianni from the Fairfield P.D."

"I've heard a lot about you, Detective Gianni. You're a bit of a legend regarding solving tough cases. I guess you want to talk about Alana Andrews. I told the detective at the scene everything, but I guess you want to hear it from me."

"That's right. Did your wife and kid see the body?"

"No. We were throwing a ball around with my son. A big

beach ball. He's only four. My wife kicked it and the wind got a hold of it and it sailed over my head into the woods. When I went to get it I saw her. I didn't know she was dead at first. So I quietly inched closer to get a better look. She was gorgeous and just sitting there, you know, bare ass, with the most incredible pair of tits I'd ever seen. I was maybe fifty feet from her when I realized that something was wrong with her. She hadn't moved an inch. I called out to her and of course there was no response. I hurried up to her and she just stared straight ahead. I waved my hands in front of her face and she didn't blink. I spoke to her and she didn't respond. She appeared to be dead. I ran back down to my wife and told her about my discovery. Then I grabbed my cell phone and called my lieutenant. I figured if I called 911 it would turn into a three-ring circus once they found out it was her. Then he told me to go back to the crime scene and keep people away until he got here. I hope I did the right thing."

"How did you know her name?"

"You kidding me? Alana Andrews was always on the entertainment shows. I recognized her immediately."

"What time was it?"

"About ten-thirty."

"Did you look around the immediate area for the murderer?"

"Not really. I did take a quick look around to see if anyone was around, but I wouldn't say I was looking for the murderer."

"Did you touch anything at the murder scene?"

"No sir!"

"You didn't check for a pulse?"

"No."

"Is the lab going to find your fingerprints on her body?"

"No way! Not that I wasn't tempted to touch her. But I didn't get any closer than about two feet."

"Did you notice if the ground seemed unusually wet near the body?"

"No."

"Prior to going into the woods, did you notice anyone leaving from that area?"

"No."

"Do you go to Lake Mohegan often?"

"Maybe a few times a year. That day was the first time this year."

"Can you think of anything else?"

"No. That's everything."

"Here's my card. If you think of anything else give me a call."

"Do you have any leads yet?"

"We've got a few people we're interested in, but were not liking anyone yet."

"You think there will be more bodies?"

"Why do you think that there will be more bodies?"

"The way she was posed and prettied up. It reminded me of a few of the case studies about serial killers at the academy."

"I like the way you think. Let's put it this way: I wouldn't be surprised if another body turned up. I've got to get back to the station. Remember to call me if you think of anything else."

"You've got it, Detective."

CHAPTER 13

Wednesday 10:00 AM

"Where do you think you're going?" Mark Peterson asked. "I'm about to make you a delicious gourmet breakfast."

"I'm not really hungry. I should get going," replied Cindee.

"Nonsense. Why do you have to go? There's no one at home waiting for you."

"Look, Mark. I don't know what got into me yesterday. I guess I was feeling lonely. You know, down and out. Feeling sorry for myself I guess. I needed someone to talk to. And, yes I do have someone at home waiting for me. My cat."

"Considering we made love three times last night, I think you wanted more from me than conversation. Now what? You're telling me you regret it?"

"No, not at all. I feel refreshed and new, but also ashamed. I'm not looking for a relationship. You're a good friend. We had a great time last night but now it's time for me to go home."

"Okay, but not until you've had your breakfast."

"Oh, all right."

Mark was pissed. Cindee showed up yesterday at his Sasco Beach mansion wearing a pair of white micro shorts and a pink halter top. Her beautiful green eyes were begging for compassion. She wanted to get laid and more. He knew it the minute he hugged her. She pressed her breasts against his chest and he could feel her nipples swell through her silk top. He was careful, though, acting like he didn't notice. He remembered the day that he photographed her in his studio. She was three years younger and just maybe the best-looking woman that he'd ever seen. She let him have her that day, too. She was young and naïve. She thought that he might have connections to help her with her career. He introduced her to Jay Martin, and he made her a star and his wife. After the introduction Mark was out of the picture. But that was okay; he got what he wanted. That's all he wanted. That's what he expected. That's what he deserved. Now she returned, needing him again, and he didn't disappoint her. He rose to the occasion three times, allowing her to orchestrate one session from start to finish. She really seemed to enjoy that, being in control of the situation. She liked to please him, too, bringing him right to the edge, but always making him wait. It's all about the control. He made up his mind that from now on he was the one in control.

"Eggs, pancakes, or French toast with your champagne?"

"Don't you have any coffee?"

"Sure. I'm going to make coffee, but you have to try my orange juice and champagne energy drink, too."

"I could use an energy drink, all right. We didn't get much sleep last night," Cindee said, and wished she hadn't. She could feel herself blushing slightly as she turned away and said softly, "French toast sounds yummy."

"French toast it is. Why don't you relax in the hot tub while I whip up breakfast?"

"Okay, but you may have to wake me."

Cindee went down the hall to the great room that housed the hot tub. Opening the door immediately brought her back to last night. The blue marble hot tub sat in a corner and the two corner walls were covered with floor-to-ceiling mirrors. Two empty wine glasses rested on the edge of the tub where they made love for the first time last night. One minute they were sitting in the hot tub naked, drinking wine, as she spilled her guts about why she was so depressed. Mark listened to every word she said and even offered her advice. She was feeling much better when Mark made his move, kissing her hard and deep. She kissed him back without hesitation, inviting him to take the next step. That was the start of a marathon love-making session like none she ever experienced. She had never made love more than twice in the same night. Her ex-husband Jay Martin was only good for a double once in a blue moon, although she often wondered if it was because he was screwing all the young bitches that hung out at their house. They hung all over him like a bunch of leaches waiting their turn for a shot at stardom. Fame and fortune would elude most of them. They loved to hang out by the pool, flaunting their young, firm bodies, often sunning themselves in the nude. He had another hot tub outside next to the pool, and it always had people in it, too. She rarely got to enjoy it with Jay or alone.

She stripped off the shirt that she had taken from Jay's closet and slipped into the water. She closed her eyes and let the water take control, massaging her body as she drifted off into a light sleep.

Jay awakened her with a kiss. "Breakfast is served, my lady." Jay had thrown a linen table cloth over the wooden cocktail table that paralleled the white leather sofa. Alongside the coffee cups and plates stood a stack of French toast, filling the air with a strong aroma of cinnamon. A dish of strawberries and a container of whipped cream sat off to the side. In the center of the table stood a vase of fresh cut flowers adding the finishing touch to a beautiful setting.

"Wow. What a great host you are, Jay."

"Oops, I forgot the coffee. I'll be right back."

Cindee climbed out of the tub and used the towel that Jay left for her to dry off. She slipped his shirt back on and sat on the edge of the sofa looking the table over again. It worried her to see the length he went through to impress her. She guessed her little speech about not wanting a relationship hadn't penetrated either of his heads.

Jay returned with a coffee pot and they proceeded to eat. "You know, last night you told me that it was you who made the moves on Tony, and I was wondering if that was the wine talking or you."

"That's the truth, I swear. I was fed up with Jay and his little harem. I told Tony about it hoping he would make a move on me, but he didn't want any part of that. He was hired to protect me, and he was too honorable a person to mess around with me. He told me that under different circumstances he wouldn't hesitate for a moment, but as long as I was married he would have to honor that union."

"So after your divorce I suppose you guys got together."

"No. He didn't seem interested anymore, and I didn't pursue it. I guess he never was interested."

Just then the phone rang and Jay answered it. "Hello? Probably in a couple of hours. Okay, I'll call you back when I'm ready. Yeah, okay."

Cindee wanted to ask him who was on the phone but instead decided to just be happy that he had someplace to go in a few hours. She assumed he'd be happy to see her leave.

They continued to eat, placing strawberries and cream on top of the French toast, savoring every bite. They were famished because they hadn't eaten dinner last night, feasting on each other instead.

"Oh, I almost forgot about our energy drinks."

"Oh don't bother, Jay, I'm stuffed."

"But I already made them. They're in the blender just waiting for the ice. Why don't you get dressed and I'll finish them up. We can drink them outside by the pool. It's like a summer day out there again. It's already seventy-seven degrees."

"Where are my clothes?"

"They're right over there on that chair," Jay said pointing to a red love seat. "I was wondering why you hadn't put them on. I don't know what happened to your panties. I guess they're around here some place."

"I don't think I was wearing any," she said as her face began to redden. *I guess I was begging for it, damn it.* "I'll see you outside."

Jay headed back to the kitchen to prepare his potent brew. The blender already contained orange and cranberry juice. All he needed to add was the champagne, a handful of ice, and Rohypnol. He careful looked over the pre-sealed bubble packs of one and two mg dose tablets that he had picked up in New Mexico a few months ago from an airport drug dealer. He added the champagne to the blender, threw in a handle full of ice cubes, and turned it on low. He enjoyed his blender. It served him well over the years. Jay peered out the window to see that Cindee was waiting patiently for him. Her sexy summer outfit was back on. He shutoff the blender and poured the mixture into two fancy crystal goblets, and decorated one with an orange peel, poking a cute little drink umbrella into it. Carefully he removed a one mg pill from the blister pack and cut it in half, placing the other half back in the package. He crushed it on the counter with a spoon, and swept it into the ornamented glass with his fingers. After all, he didn't want to knock her out. He just wanted to make her ready, willing, and able to feast upon another marathon of sexual delights. When used properly, the date-rape drug was a please-have-your-way-with-me drug. That thought reminded him that he might need a little pharmaceutical help himself after last night's escapade. He jogged up to his bedroom and found his stash of little blue pills. He swallowed one without hesitation, knowing that there was no way he was going to satisfy two women without it. Before heading out to the pool he called Mya Bates to tell her it was time to come over.

CHAPTER 14

Wednesday 2:30 PM

Mark and Cindee were still outside when Mya arrived. Mya was a stunning thirty-one-year-old exotic beauty, born of a black father and Hawaiian mother. She was an actress wannabe who left home at the ripe old age of twenty-two, moving to California to pursue an acting career. She soon learned that the competition was brutal and embarked on a crusade to become educated, and became an attorney instead. To fund her schooling she worked as an exotic dancer for the Hollywood Room, a well known California strip club. She eventually moved east and graduated Law School from Quinnipiac University in Hamden, CT. She continued to work at strip clubs in nearby Stamford and New York City while attending law school. Now she was in private practice and currently representing several celebrities for contract disputes and libel suits.

She let herself in through the front door with the key that Mark hid below one of the garage windows. She found the nearly empty blender in the kitchen, added more champagne and ice, and turned it on. A few granules of the little white pill on the counter brought a smile to her face. *This should be a fun afternoon!* She shut off the blender, poured the mixture into a crystal goblet that was on the counter, and headed out to the pool.

"Hi," said Mya as she approached them. "You must be Cindee Cox. I loved you on the soaps. I'm Mark's friend, Mya."

"Hi. Thank you. Thank you very much."

"So what are you guys up to?"

"We're just hanging out and enjoying the summer-like weather after a fantastic night of sex," Mark replied with a wide devilish smile.

"Mark!"

"It's okay, Cindee," Mya assured her. "Mark and I are old friends, and we discuss our sex lives on a regular basis."

Cindee was at a loss for words as the Rohypnol began to work its devilish magic and cloud her brain. "I'm really starting to feel that drink, except I think you may have overdone it on the champagne. Is it getting hotter out here by the minute, or is it just me?"

Mya and Mark laughed as Mya pulled off her sundress, revealing her well-toned, naked body. At five foot six and one hundred and ten pounds, she was perfect. Her olive skin glowed in the sunlight as her brown hair with red highlights took on a life of their own. Mya's large, deep-brown nipples complemented her well-toned body.

"You're shaved clean down there," Cindee said as she touched Mya's pubic area.

"Yeah, I like that clean look, and it makes quite a statement, don't you think? Would you like me to help you shave yours?"

"Maybe later," Cindee said. "I'm going to sit in the spa,

Mya. Care to join me?" Cindee started her descend into the hot water.

"Sure. You going in with your clothes on?" Mya asked.

"I guess I'm not thinking straight. It must be the champagne," she said as she shimmied her white shorts down to her ankles, revealing a neatly cropped pubic area.

"Let me help you. Place your hands on my shoulder while I get them off. I don't want you to slip."

"Thanks, Mya. The top is easy. See?" she said as she pulled it off over her head and threw it in Mark's direction before slipping into the water.

"Mark?"

"You two go ahead, Mya. I'll join you in a few minutes."

As soon as she was seated, Mya moved the goblets out of harm's way. "Don't you just love the feel of the bubbling water on your body?"

"Yeah," Cindee replied giggling. "And if you straddle a water jet like this you can give yourself an unbelievable orgasm."

While Cindee pleasured herself with the stream of water Mya got behind her and ran her hands over her breasts.

"Oh, oh, God, that feels so good. You want to try it?"

"I've got a better idea." Mya easily lifted her up and sat her on the edge of the spa.

"Hmm. Nothing like the real thing," Cindee cooed as Mya replaced the water jet with her tongue.

Mark was naked now, too, sporting his rock-hard nine-inch penis like a prized trophy.

"Wow, don't you look good," Mya said as she grabbed his manhood. "Viagra?"

"Yeah. I had to. We did it three times last night, and I don't want to disappoint either of you today, although you seem to be doing just fine without me."

Mya pulled him into the spa by his penis and guided it within inches of Cindee's face. Cindee gave the tip of his penis a kiss and then leaned back to enjoy Mya's advances.

"Easy, Mark," Mya advised as he tried to encourage Cindee to engage him. "Why don't we go up to your bedroom and really show Miss Cindee a good time?"

"Are you game, Cindee?"

Her mouth moved but the words didn't vocalize. She was dizzy and disoriented. He grabbed a handful of her hair on the top of her head and bobbed her head up and down.

"Looks like a yes to me, Mya. Do you agree?"

"Let's go explore the possibilities, Mark."

CHAPTER 15

Wednesday 7:30 PM

Brenda was growing quite impatient with Doctor Crowe. She spent about an hour preparing for his arrival and was ready at seven-thirty. She was wearing a cute V-necked, yellow top she dug out from her summer clothes and a pair of white, low-hung jeans that made her ass look great. Even at thirty-five she could go braless, bare her belly, and look better than some women ten years younger. Doctor Crowe arrived about eight o'clock.

"Hi, Darren," she said as she took the bag of Chinese food from him and brought it into the kitchen.

"Sorry I'm late."

"No kidding. Let's eat. I'm starving. Would you like a beer or some wine?"

"I'll have whatever you're having."

"Then beer it is."

Brenda set up two plates with the Moo Goo Gai Pan, fried

rice, and a shrimp egg roll, and brought them out to the deck. They ate in silence, enjoying the view of the water.

"I'll have the DNA results from the semen in the morning," said Darren, breaking the silence.

"Good. I can't wait to run them through the FBI files for a match."

"Did you find out anything about those dildos?"

"Those dildos could have been purchased online or at a variety of locations. I brought one over to Pleasant Dreams for them to look at, and they told me that it was a very standard item."

"Standard? Ten inches long and what? Two or three inches around is standard? Did they say how many they sell a year?"

"About five hundred, including what they sell on their website."

"Holy shit...five hundred a year. And that's just one company. Imagine how many are sold throughout the world! "I'll have Lois run some searches tomorrow and see if any of the popular websites have received orders of two or more. I have to believe that the typical horny housewife doesn't order more than one ten-inch dildo at a time."

"You want to hear something strange?"

"What now? They sold twice as many fifteen-inch dildos?"

"Ha...that's funny, but no."

"I noticed that the skin around her pubic area and thighs had a slight rash. I sent some skin scrapings off to the lab and the preliminary report indicates very early signs of pediculosis corporis, commonly known as body lice."

"What!"

"Yeah that's what I thought. Why would a woman like her have lice? But after some thought, I believe that one of the men who raped her had lice."

"That's it, Darren," she said as she grabbed the plates and

brought them to the sink. "You have managed to completely ruin my appetite. I invited you over to cheer me up, and instead you brought me back down."

"I'm sorry. I should have waited and told you tomorrow. I thought you wanted to know everything as soon as I found out."

"It's not your fault. You could make it up to me with a massage. My neck and shoulders are so damn tight you could run a bow across them and play Beethoven."

"Sure, my pleasure. How about a little Bach, too?"

"Smartass!" Brenda lifted her top off as she walked to the hot tub, being careful to only give him a glimpse of her breasts. Once there she kept her back to him and slipped out of her tight, white jeans revealing a white lace thong that exemplified her butt. "Stop staring at it. Grab the wine, and get your ass over here, maestro," she cooed as she stepped into the water.

"Nice underwear," Darren said as he approached with the bottle and two glasses, handing one over to her.

"Shush up, and get your ass in the water. I'm ready for my massage," she said, turning her back to him as her breasts appeared to be floating on top of the water. "And if your performance is bravura, I'll send you home with a big smile on your face, virtuoso."

CHAPTER 16

Thursday 8:00 AM

Frank and Brenda put their heads together in the morning and compared notes. They had nothing as far as suspects were concerned. Frank had viewed the DVD last night and was also appalled with the events that took place. Brenda told him all about what Darren had said, and they agreed that Lois should use her internet skills to get them more information about the murder weapon.

"Let's take a closer look at the rapists. One of those assholes must have had lice," Frank said.

"I don't want to look at it again, Frank. You do it."

Brenda grabbed a photo of the dildo and went over to see Lois to explain what she wanted her to do.

"My God," Lois gasped. "That's a huge one. And you say it's a big seller?"

"Five hundred sold by Pleasant Dreams alone."

"Wow! I wonder how many the V.I.P. franchises sell."

"Just get me a report of who bought two or more from websites and local stores."

"I'll get right on it."

The desk clerk called over to Brenda to say she had a phone call. "A Mrs. Pucho."

"Transfer it over here. Yes, Mrs. Pucho, this is Detective Corrino. What can I do for you?"

Mrs. Pucho was concerned because Cindee Cox hadn't returned home from her bike ride.

"Has she ever done that before?"

"Well, yes, but I'm concerned because that other actress was killed a few days ago."

"Let's give it a little more time. She may be staying with a friend. Call me back tomorrow whether she shows up or not."

"Okay."

"Brenda, I viewed the DVD again. You don't get much of a look at their equipment. Maybe the lab can do some video enhancements. The only thing that stood out to me was that the men's clothes looked worn and a bit tattered."

"All of them."

"All except the murderer."

"Interesting," she said and told him about Mrs. Pucho's phone call.

"I guess it could mean something, and then again it could be nothing. How did you leave off with her?"

"I told her to call me back tomorrow whether she shows up or not."

"Good. I didn't get anything new from the Easton rookie, either. Oh, and McMillan said that the wet ground was consistent with the lake water. So I don't know if the murderer went down to the water to wash something off his hands or what. There are footprints but no fingerprints."

"Hey, Brenda," shouted Lois. "A quick search gave me hundreds of hits. They also have a strap-on version. Should I check that one, too?"

"Check both, I guess, and concentrate on local shops first and then spread out a little. Remember. Find out who's ordered more than one."

Brenda's phone rang, and she answered, "Detective Corrino."

"Is this the symphony organist? I was wondering if I could catch your next gig."

"Sounds like you're still smiling. What's up?"

"Remember the body lice that I told you about? The final report points to a condition that is common among homeless people."

"Homeless people?"

"That doesn't necessarily mean the rapists are homeless people, but they could have had close contact with a homeless person and got infested with that type of lice."

"Okay, thanks."

"Any plans for the weekend?"

"I'm working."

"Figures."

"What's that supposed to mean?"

"Nothing. Forget about it. Thanks for the info."

Brenda told Frank about the body lice and homeless people connection.

"I guess there could be something to it, but when are homeless people involved in something like this? Raping a movie star? Wouldn't they be raping their own kind?"

"I guess it could be a person that had sex with a homeless person and got infested with the bugs."

"Who in their right mind would have sex with a filthy person, unless it was an unplanned rape, and once he started he was going to shoot his load no matter what."

"Let's get a few of the guys to check some of the usual places where the homeless hang out and see if anyone knows anything. Better have them check Bridgeport, too."

"Well, it's been a few days and we haven't had another body. I think you owe me lunch. Remember, there wasn't any evidence that she was sodomized, either."

"Not so fast, lady. I was right about the piercing and the rape. As soon as another body shows up, I'll be seventy-five percent correct. Then I win."

"You're a winner, all right. Like that's going to happen, too."

"It ain't over till it's over."

CHAPTER 17

Thursday 2:00 PM

The rest of the day was uneventful, and both Frank and Brenda were feeling a little burned out and really needed a day off. Since that wasn't an option they both decided to leave a little early and steal a few hours. Frank's youngest son Michael was performing in a school play in the afternoon, so he couldn't get into anything too deep if he wanted to see it. He enjoyed doing things with his family but rarely had the time. He tried to put them first but being a cop didn't always make it possible. Frank called home to let Marie know that he'd be home in time for them to all go together.

"Great! How'd you make that happen?" asked Marie.

"We're kind of stuck between a rock and a hard place right now. We don't have any really good suspects, and nothing new is happening with the investigation. I decided it might be a good idea to get away from it for a while.

"Tomorrow we'll have a little bit more to work on, and we'll be fresh. I'll see you in about an hour."

"Okay."

While Frank was spending some quality time with Marie and the kids, Brenda was trying to catch up on some sleep but couldn't. Too many things on her mind. Her dates with Darren troubled her. She was being too damn forward and promiscuous. She's been asking him out and luring him with sex. *Maybe I'm not attractive enough. Maybe I'm too damn easy. Give me a massage and I'll send you home with a smile on your face. What the hell was I thinking?* Brenda did finally drift off to sleep but her mind remained restless as it replayed the choking scene over and over again. What made matters worse was that the woman in her dream was her. She was naked and tied to the bed but she wasn't wearing a mask. Then the murderer entered the room and straddled her chest. Neither of them spoke because she knew it was useless. No one would hear her, and soon the torture would be over. He didn't remove his mask before he began to work the dildo into her throat. In and out, up and down, but she was not choking. In fact, she was enjoying it. Soon she was swallowing the whole ten inches and laughing in his face. In and out, up and down. Over and over again. Finally the murderer realized that he couldn't kill her with it so he stopped. He gave up. It was surreal. She laughed a deep victory laugh and woke up drenched with perspiration. *I am too damn easy!*

Brenda had a decent childhood. Her mother was a school teacher and her father was an operations manager at a commercial printing company. They brought her up properly. She didn't let boys get past second base until after she graduated high school. The summer before she started college she fell in love with a boy two years her senior while working at a summer camp. He showed her how to party and eventually convinced her to let him have her. After that summer he dumped her, and Brenda was a different person. In college she was the pursuer and had plenty of action but never love. She couldn't find Mr. Right, and he never showed up to sweep her off her feet, either. But that was okay because she was in charge now. She was the boss, and she would do the dumping. Guys weren't going to take advantage of her anymore unless she wanted them to.

Meanwhile Frank, Marie, Frank Jr., and Cybil sat in the school auditorium enjoying the play and Michael's performance. Frank's mind drifted off to Marie and their sex life. *It's been about two weeks since I've gotten laid. This damn case is taking up too much of my time. I get home late and Marie is too tired. I've got to catch those bastard's before my marriage goes to shit!*

"Hon, why don't we stop at the Southport Brewing Factory to grab a bite on the way home?" Frank asked.

"You know, I'd love to, but not with the kids. I wish you and I could find some time to go out to dinner. It seems like ages since we had some time together without the kids, not to mention getting together, period. I can't remember the last time I saw you naked."

"Yeah, I know."

"How about letting me see it tonight?"

"Really? Do I need to bring you a thick juicy steak from the restaurant?"

"I'll settle for a thick juicy sausage instead."

They shared a laugh and held hands. Frank's penis was hard, and he steered Marie's hand so that it grazed alongside it. She gave him a nervous stare and grinned but didn't try to pull away. He knew he was getting some tonight.

CHAPTER 18

Friday 9:00 AM

Brenda wondered where Frank was this morning. He's rarely ever late. Finally he showed up about nine o'clock looking a little tired.

"What did you do, get some last night?"

Frank ignored her.

She looked right into his eyes and said, "You did, didn't you!"

Frank fought off a smile but the smile won out as he tried to speak.

"No need to answer now," Brenda said perceiving that a smile and no acknowledgement meant she was right.

"Frank, I had a voice mail from Mrs. Pucho. Cindee Cox is back home. She heard a car door slam about ten-thirty last night, and by the time she got to the window she could see the lights were on next-door."

"We should stop there today since we know she's home. I'm

real curious to hear her version of the Jay Martin and Tony Perceo story."

"Yeah, before she goes off on another two-day bicycle ride."

*

They headed out just before noon and stopped at the Center Deli for lunch, a regular lunch stop when you're near headquarters. Frank ordered a roast beef and cheese on rye, one of his favorites. Brenda went for a salad with slices of grilled chicken on top.

"Watching your figure again?" Frank asked.

"If I don't watch it, nobody else will watch it either!"

"You and the Doc getting serious?"

"I don't think so." Brenda said with a touch of aloofness and a little hurt in her voice.

The mood switched from friendly to ice cold. They ate in silence. Frank'd been married long enough to know when he'd said something that'd hit a sour note. He was just trying to make some non-work conversation. Something they didn't do very often. Better to keep quiet and let it wear off. Soon they'd be back to the business at hand.

*

Cindee Cox awakened at eleven o'clock feeling hung over. She ached from head to toe. She was a little groggy when she stood naked in front of her full length admiring herself. *They are so damn beautiful, and thanks to Mother Nature they didn't cost me a dime. Not like some of the whores I work with, buying the best boobs money can buy.* Continuing to admire her sexy body her eyes focused on her vagina. "What the hell? Where's my hair? That asshole shaved off all my pubic hair! He must have! Why don't I remember?" She admired the new look, swirling a finger around the perimeter of her vagina, noticing it was a little tender. She grabbed the phone and dialed Mark's number. *What happened to my pubic hair?*

Mya and Mark were in bed lightly nibbling on each other when the phone rang.

"Hello?" Mark answered.

"Why did you shave off my pubic hair?"

"I didn't."

"Bullshit!"

"You asked Mya to do it because you like her shaved look. Don't you remember? Don't you like it?"

"I vaguely remember her. I guess I like it. Did she make love to me?"

"We both did. Don't you remember?" asked Mark as Mya began to knead his manhood between her breasts.

"You, me, and Mya. You mean the three of us at the same time?"

"Yeah."

"Why don't I remember? I'd remember something like that."

"I guess the hot sun along with drinks went to your head. Hmm," Mark involuntarily moaned as Mya kissed the tip of his penis.

"God damn it, Mark! Are you in bed with her right now?"

"Yeah. You woke us up."

"Did you sodomize me?"

"What?"

"You heard me. Did you sodomize me?"

"I don't remember. I may have. Yeah, probably."

"God damn it, Mark! What the hell is wrong with you? Did I tell you to do that? Did I give you permission to do it? I'm not a freaking whore or some porno queen. I don't do that! I've never done that. And I don't have sex with two people at the same time, either!"

"I honestly don't remember whose idea it was. We were all just having a good time. You and Mya took turns with me, and then she rubbed that strawberry gel on us and it just happened. I guess you didn't mind because of all the lubrication. You didn't ask me to stop. In fact you enjoyed it. Before that I watched you and Mya go at it. I think that was when you asked her to shave you. You said you wanted to have a nice smoothie like hers."

"I said that? I never did anything with a woman before in my life nor had a threesome either. I don't know what got into me. How did I get home?"

"I took you home last night about ten. You don't remember that either?"

"I'm not sure. I kind of do. I don't know. About yesterday... I hope Mya doesn't think I'm a slut. You didn't tell her I was there the day before, too, did you?"

"Yeah, she knows, but it's okay. That's why she wanted to come over. I told her how beautiful you were and about your great sexy body. She's a bisexual. We have that kind of a relationship. I wanted her to enjoy you, too."

"I've got to go," she said as she hung up the phone, quite disgusted with herself.

*

Mya straddled Mark and inserted his manhood inside, riding him once again.

"I swear, Mya; you're going to wear me out. I need to save something for next weekend."

"I just want to enjoy you again before I go home. I take it that was Miss Cindee. Maybe she could join us in New York sometime?"

"I doubt it. Cindee didn't sound like she enjoyed our little orgy. Hell, she doesn't even remember any of it," Jay said as he began laughing.

Mya began laughing, too, as she rode Mark to yet another climax.

CHAPTER 19

Friday 1:00 PM

Cindee soaked in a bubble bath filled with Celine Dion bath oil for a good half hour, carefully washing her abused openings, trying desperately to remember the threesome with Mark and Mya. She could only visualize bits and pieces, confusing one day with the next, as though she lost a day of her life. The beautiful fragrance of Celine Dion sweetened the air. She dozed off for a few minutes and was awakened by her front doorbell. She didn't have a bathrobe with her, so she draped a towel from front to back, holding the opening in the back with her hand, and headed for the front door. She peaked through the peep hole and saw a man and a woman, the man raising his hand to knock on the door.

"Can I help you?" Cindee inquired.

"We are Fairfield Police detectives. We'd like to ask you a few questions."

Fear shot through her body. *Yesterday's orgy. Is it against the law to participate in an orgy? Should I tell them I was drunk and didn't know what I was doing? How could they know about it?*

"About what?"

"Jay Martin, Tony Perceo, and Alana Andrews."

"Oh...okay. You'll have to wait a few minutes. I have to get dressed. You caught me in the bath. Give me a few minutes."

"Okay."

Cindee headed for the bedroom, the towel barely covering her ass. She threw on a pair of pink sweats and a "Save the Seals" tee-shirt over her naked body. She checked herself out in the mirror. *I look like shit.* She quickly applied some eye shadow and a fresh coat of Spiderman-red lipstick. She grabbed a hairbrush and tried to straighten out her greasy hair, but the steam from the bath had kinked it. She noticed that the ends were wet from sitting in the water. *Oh well!* She decided to put it in a ponytail. She stumbled and almost fell as she rushed back to the front door, realizing that she was a little unstable.

She opened the door and said, "Hi. May I see your IDs?"

They showed their IDs and followed her into a sparsely furnished, mundane living room with a colonial theme. *A far cry from Jay Martin's majestic spread in Greenfield Hill.*

"Please sit down. Now what do Tony and Jay have to do with Alana's death?"

"Were not sure," replied Brenda. "We were hoping that you could tell us."

"No. Jay may be an asshole, but Alana meant money to him, and money means everything to Jay. The more money he has, the more women he can have hanging all over him. Tony...he's too nice and a real gentleman."

"Are you aware that Tony was a detective with NYPD?"

"Of course."

"Was Tony Perceo the reason why you and Jay split?" Brenda asked.

"That was a large part of the problem, but we had other issues, too."

"Would you mind telling me where you've been for the past two days?" Frank inquired.

"I was at a friend's house."

"Someone nearby?"

"Yeah, down by Sasco Beach. What does my personal life have to do with any of this?"

"Probably nothing. Your neighbor was worried about you."

"Who, Mrs. Pucho? She worries about everything. Then let's just leave it at that and talk about something else."

"Okay. Were you and Tony Perceo lovers?" asked Brenda.

"No. If it was up to me we would have been. He's everything that Jay isn't. Look, I'm tired and need to take a nap. Are you through with the questions?"

"Just a few more. What's your friend's name?" asked Frank.

"Mark Alexander."

"What kind of a car does he drive?"

"A silver Audi. One of those Roadsters."

"One last question, Miss Cox. Did he bring you home last night?"

"Yeah, that's right. Why?"

"We saw a car like that up at Mr. Martins' house, and when we ran the plates it was registered to a business called Celebrity Sightings Inc. Is Mark Alexander Celebrity Sightings?"

"That's him. He's a professional photographer. He does portfolios for potential actresses and models. He posts some of the pictures on his website free of charge."

"Interesting," said Brenda. "Did he ever photograph you or Alana Andrews?"

"Yeah. Both of us. I recommended him to her. His portfolio package is reasonably priced compared to the New York City photographers, and he's local."

"Why do so many soap opera stars live in Fairfield?" asked Frank.

"Economics. It costs about three times as much to live in the city, and you get much less for your money. Plus there's a lot more privacy here."

"Where is Alexander's studio?" Frank asked.

"At his house. Now please. How many more last questions do you have? I'm really tired."

"I'm sorry," said Brenda. "Did Alana ever mention that she was being stalked?"

"No. I hadn't seen her for quite some time. Did you find out who it was?"

"We didn't know about it. Tony Perceo was her bodyguard."

"Tony! Really. I didn't know he was working for her."

Cindee's anguish was enough for them to finally leave her to her nap. She had quite enough of their questions.

"Okay, Ms. Cox," said Frank. "We appreciate the time you've given us. We'll be on our way."

Back in the car they talked about how tired she looked. "She looked like she was partying all night," said Frank. "Probably doing coke or something."

"Maybe, but I think there was more to it than that. You don't spend two days with a guy and not get any. I know what she was feeling. I think she was physically and emotionally exhausted." A soft, pretty smile began to form across her face as she closed her eyes and thought about Doctor Darren and their hot-tub escapades.

CHAPTER 20

Friday 10:00 PM

"I love this place, don't you?" Mya said as she and Mark entered the Pleasure Chest, a private sex club located in Vista, New York, a rural area just over the Connecticut border. The man inside the entrance door of the plain exterior building was built like a young Arnold Schwarzenegger and stood completely naked except for a black bowtie on a ring fitted snugly around his penis and attached to a black thong. Both of his pierced nipples sported Pleasure Chest-logoed jewelry engraved onto a simple treasure chest design. The word "Welcum" was written in crimson lipstick on his stomach, centered perfectly above the bowtie. He asked if they were members or if it was a first time visit.

"New guy at the gate, huh," Mark said as he flashed his membership card to the man.

"Yeah, he's new but not that new. I guess you haven't been here recently."

"Yeah. It's time to recharge our batteries," Mya said with a big smile.

The man opened the interior door that led into a small foyer. The floor was green marble, and the walls were done with floral wallpaper on the top two-thirds and lime green sponge painting on the rest. Over in the far corner a man was getting a blowjob. The woman was kneeling on a sapphire colored bra, one knee on each cup. They appeared to be in their mid-forties.

"I think that's against the club rules," Mark said lightheartedly to the couple.

She stopped immediately and the man replied, "It is? I'm sorry, we're new. We assumed that anything goes in a place like this. We were just trying to fit in."

"That's pretty much the case," Mark said, "but come on, not in the fucking entranceway. At least go inside and put your clothes away. Then you'll have your choice of a private room, an orgy room, or anything in between to do whatever you want. Are you looking to swap with another couple?"

"We don't know," the man replied nervously. "My name is Jack, and this is my wife Karen," he said offering his hand to shake.

Before Mark or Mya could answer Karen said, "Jack has grown to be a little conservative over time, but I'm planning on experiencing the whole nine yards. In fact I might even try a woman. I don't know. Just the thought of this place has me as horny as Cleopatra! Women do get together here, don't they?"

Mark and Mya laughed at her enthusiasm as Mya helped her up to her feet. "Through that door are the locker rooms, one for the men and one for the women. You can grab a towel or robe to wear if you didn't bring anything to change into. Since it's your first time, I don't suggest walking around naked until you decide what you're willing to do."

Sensing Karen's apprehension, she grabbed her by the arm and steered her towards the ladies locker room.

"We'll see you guys in the bar," Mya said as Karen dropped some of her clothes. As she bent over to pick them up Mya noticed Mark eyeing Karen's rear and gave him a smile of approval.

In the locker room Mya explained that every locker housed an oriental, designer-silk robe and two towels.

Mya said, "Hang your clothes and stuff in a locker that has a key. Make sure the key works before you close it. You can wear as little or as much as you want. You can always come back and add or subtract. Take the key and attach it to your bar bracelet like this. Each bracelet has four beads, and each bead will buy you a drink at the bar. They don't have any hard liquor but they do have wine, beer, juice, or soda."

"Are you and your husband regulars?"

"We're not married, and yeah, we have an annual membership, but we don't visit as often as we'd like to. So how long have you two been married?"

"Twenty-five years this month. This visit is our anniversary gift to each other. Something we always wanted to try. Now that our kids are on their own we decided to make it happen. I told him we're not getting any younger. So if we're going to do it let's do it while we are still in pretty good shape. Are most of the people that come here young like you?"

"Actually, it's a mixed bag. I've seen them as young as eighteen and as old as seventy. All shapes and sizes, too. You'll fit in just fine."

"Wow! What do you usually wear in the club?"

"A thong."

"That's it? Why bother?"

"I think I look sexier in a thong than totally naked, and as long as it is on it tells the men that they have to ask. Besides, I want to leave something to imagination."

"What do you think I should wear, it being my first time?"

"If I had a pair like yours I'd wear the half towel fastened at the waist."

"Yeah, boobs that are sagging closer to the floor as we speak."

"They look great to me. Well, you can wear your bra, but I suggest you don't. If you get involved with somebody it will get in the way and probably get lost. A lot depends on how soon and how much action you want. You can always leave on your street clothes and just be an observer."

"Yeah, I wondered if I'd chicken out. Wearing clothes would make it easy for me to do just that."

"Trust me, and go with the half towel. It has a Velcro closure so it's easy to work on and off. Go for it. Have fun. That's why you're here, right?"

Karen removed all of her clothes and put the half towel on. She turned to face Mya.

"Do you really think my boobs are great?"

"Believe me, they'll be a hit," replied Mya as she grabbed Karen's nipples and gave them a hard twist. They responded to her touch and became erect in her fingers. "They'll love them. I know I do."

Karen closed her eyes, enjoying the moment. Mya took advantage of the situation and placed her mouth over one nipple, gently taking it between her lips, while thrusting two fingers into Karen's vagina. Karen opened her eyes and asked Mya to kiss her. She kissed her all right, sticking her tongue deep into her mouth. Mya continued toying with her nipples while explaining what to expect in the club.

"This is the kind of foreplay you can expect in the bar. There'll be some licking and sucking as well, but it's usually kept to a minimum. No serious sex, just a lot of teasing. From there you can take someone to a cubicle built for two. If you want a mini orgy go into one of the larger cubicles and you'll soon be joined by others. Or join one already in progress. The main room is called the Roman Empire, and it's where the wild, anything-goes action takes place. But you don't have to participate. You can always just enjoy watching, although I'll tell you from experience that if you watch too long you'll soon be joining the action. So are you ready to do what you've waited twenty-five years to do?"

"Yeah, I think so."

"Then let's go into the bar and see what the men are up to."

Karen stayed close to Mya as they passed through the door of the Foreplay Lounge. Jack and Mark were standing near the end of the bar. A pretty, small-framed brunette dressed in a Pleasure Chest robe was sitting on a barstool between them. She held one penis in each hand. They were all drinking red wine and talking to each other as the woman teased them along.

"Hey guys," Mya said as she approached the threesome. The woman looked towards Mya but never lost a beat.

"Mya, this is Jane," Mark said referring to the brunette.

"Hi, Jane, this is my friend Karen."

Jane's eyes focused on Karen's breasts, and she reached out to touch them, letting the men off her leash.

"Nice, and real, too," she said. You two belong to these two stiffs?" she said with a devilish grin.

"Well, we came here with them, if that's what you mean," replied Karen.

"Well, let me get out of your way," Jane said as she got up and headed towards a door with a sign above it that read, THE ROMAN EMPIRE. "Maybe we'll bump into each other later."

"So, I see you found some action already," Karen said to Jack.

"Yeah. This place is something else, isn't it?"

"You haven't seen anything yet," Mya said as she bent over and gave Jack's penis a lick and a kiss. She stood up and gave Mark a nice sexy kiss on the lips before she turned to Karen and pinched her nipples again. Mark cupped Mya's breasts and flicked his fingers across her nipples, too. Not to be left out, Jack placed his hands on Mya's beautiful firm ass and softly kneaded her cheeks.

"Shall we enter the Roman Empire now, Karen or do you want to have a drink?" asked Mya as she continued to play with Karen's nipples.

"I'm ready to go in now," she cooed, obviously enjoying the attention.

"Now look," Mark said as they headed towards the door. "Don't take this the wrong way, but I think you and Jack should go your own way, instead of following us around. That's the best way to experience this place. I'm sure we'll bump into each other later, and maybe we'll finish what we started."

They entered the Roman Empire, and it was obvious that this was the orgy room. About seventy-five percent of the people were completely naked and about half of them were having one-on-one sex right out in the open. A few groups of three or more, could be seen scattered about. The room was about two hundred feet long and one hundred feet wide, with several large ceiling fans slowly turning. The walls were tiled on the lower half and painted white above with many mirrors, paintings and photographs of nature. Along the walls were different-sized cubicles, some occupied with many people involved in an orgy. Three Jacuzzis, one in the middle of the room and one on each end, were full of naked people. They were large enough for twenty people to soak at once. On the floor there were many king-sized mattresses laid next to each other with walkways every so often so you could cross to the other side without disturbing the people that were having sex. Every so often there was a live tree growing out of the floor, some as tall as the ceiling. Jazz music bellowed from the many ceiling speakers located throughout the room.

"Did I mention that only foreplay is allowed in the Jacuzzi? If you do more than that they will ask you to leave. Other wise you can pretty much do whatever you want, to whoever you want, unless they say no," instructed Mya.

"Who would come to a place like this and say no?" asked Jack.

"If Mark wanted to do you Greek, would you let him, Jack?"

"Hell no! I'm not into men."

"How about you, Karen? Would you let him sodomize you?"

"No. I'm not into that either."

"Well, then, I think that answers the no question," said Mya. "Now you two run along and have fun. Remember, you do not have to have sex with anyone."

Mya gave Karen a love pat on the ass, and she and Mark headed towards the middle of the room.

"So, what do you want to do, Karen?" asked Jack.

"Let's walk around and watch for a while. If we see something good we could just join in, I guess."

As they walked away, Mya asked Mark, "Nice couple, don't you think?"

"Yeah. I think I'd do her."

"Me, too!"

CHAPTER 21

Saturday, April 24, 2004, 10:30 AM

Brenda was only at her desk for a few hours, trying to make some sense out of the case when she got some disturbing news. A guy was walking his dog at Lake Mohegan this morning when he came upon a naked woman sitting in the middle of the woods. She was a gorgeous redhead, and his first instinct was to get down low and admire her for a while. But his dog refused to sit still longer than a few seconds, and started to make noise as he tried to break his hold. Rather than getting caught at being a voyeur he stood up and called out to her. *Miss? Are you okay?* She didn't answer. *Miss? Can I help you?* She didn't move. He approached her and when he stood right in front of her she didn't as much as blink.

Brenda called Frank on his cell phone as she headed towards the lake. "Where are you, Frank?"

"I'm on my way in. What's up?"

"I think I owe you lunch."

"No Shit. Another body turned up?"

"Yeah, this morning, and it sounds like the same M.O."

"Are you on your way there?"

"Yeah."

"I'll be there in about ten minutes. If you get there first, keep everybody away from the crime scene until I get there."

Brenda did arrive first. Three patrol cars were in the parking lot and a couple of patrolmen were guarding the entrance into the park. Up on the hill, in the same area that they found the first victim, a few more patrolmen were visible.

"Good morning, Detective," said the patrolman guarding the entrance gate.

Brenda didn't recognize him. "Good morning. Where's the guy that found the body?" Brenda asked.

"He's inside sitting on a park bench. I told him he would have to hang around until a detective interviewed him."

"What's his name?"

"Hank Proseki."

"Thanks. Would you do me a favor and go up to the murder scene and tell them that Detective Gianni is on his way here and he asked that they don't move anything until he gets here? Then come back down to the gate and don't let anyone through here unless they're one of us," she said as she entered the park and found Mr. Proseki digging a hole in the sand with his feet.

"Mr. Proseki?" she said in his direction.

"Yes. That's me."

Hank Proseki was about fifty-five years old, and wore a blue Yankees cap, gray sweatshirt, and blue jeans. His face was a bit weathered but not like a construction worker.

"I'm Detective Corrino. I understand you found the body."

"Yeah. I was walking my dog, Pluto."

"Do you come here often?"

"No"

"Why today?"

"I don't know. I just decided to come here this morning."

"Don't you work?"

"I took an early retirement from the post office."

"Would you mind showing me where you were walking when you discovered the body?"

"Yeah sure." He got up and began to walk up the hill several hundred feet. "Come on, Pluto. We were right about here when I first saw her. I thought I died and went to heaven. About fifty feet right in front of me sat a gorgeous woman, and she was stark naked. My first instinct was to crouch down and spy on her. We were both kind of camouflaged from each other by the brush and trees. I figured she must be there with a guy. He's probably, you know, urinating in the woods or something."

"So what were you expecting, a sex show?"

"I didn't mean anything by it. I don't know. I was just curious. I was just looking when Pluto decided he didn't want to sit still anymore. I was worried that she would see me first and accuse me of spying on her, and her boyfriend would come after me. So I called out to her as I walked towards her. I walked right up to her. She never moved. I figured she must be dead."

"You married, Hank?"

"I was. I'm a widower."

"Did you touch her?"

"No, ma'am."

"You sure? She's a beautiful, naked woman. You didn't want to touch her?"

"Well, sure I wanted to touch her, but I didn't. I swear."

"Did you see or hear anyone?"

"No."

"Did you notice anything unusual?"

"Well, I did find it kind of strange that the ground around her was wet."

"What do you mean, like puddles?"

"No just wet, like grass early in the morning."

"Is that why your knees are stained?"

"I just kneeled in front of her so I could look directly into her eyes, that's all."

Brenda was sure he was lying, but it didn't really matter how closely he examined her, as long as he didn't touch her. "All right, Hank. I'll need your address and phone number in case I need to speak with you again. Then you can leave."

Brenda wrote the information into her notebook and went up to examine the body. She recognized her to be Candie Street, a model who'd seen limited work and aspired to make it as a film actress. Brenda remembered seeing her either on Jay Leno or Letterman within the past month or so. She told the crime scene personnel to take ground samples around the body and to find out what caused the dampness. She forced herself to look at her face. A dildo was stuck in her throat, just like Alana Andrews. Her beautiful blue eyes were staring straight out towards the woods. Her hands were tied around her back and to the same tree. Her breasts were large but appeared to be natural. The nipples sported the same gold nipple jewelry. She ordered a patrolman to cut her loose from the tree and turned her on her side to reveal the second dildo. Based on the duplication, she conceded that Frank was right. A serial killer may be running loose in Fairfield after all.

Frank had arrived and was walking up the hill towards her when her cell phone rang.

"Corrino."

"Brenda, it's Lois. That Martin guy thinks there's another DVD in his mailbox."

"Call him back and tell him not to touch it. I'll be there in ten minutes to pick it up."

"Pick what up?" Frank asked.

"That was Lois. Jay Martin called to tell me he found another strange package in his mailbox. I'm going to run over there and pick it up before the asshole messes with it. I'm guessing it's another DVD. I took a quick look at the body. She's a model trying to get into films. Her name is Candie Street. It looks like the same M.O."

Frank could see the body was on its side. "Damn it. They cut the rope and moved her."

"I moved her."

"Why did you move her? I didn't want anything disturbed."

"You're not the only detective working this case. I apologize if I got carried away doing my job."

"I'll finish up here," Frank said, obviously pissed off. "I'll see you back at the station."

Brenda practically bumped into Dr. Crowe as she walked through the parking lot towards her car.

"Hey," said Darren. "What's the rush?"

"Looks like the same M.O. and there may be another DVD of the murder. I'm heading over to pick it up. Frank's up there taking care of business."

"Oh joy, my favorite homicide detective."

"Hey. I thought I was your favorite detective."

"You're my favorite female homicide detective," he said giving her a peck on the cheek after a quick survey of who was in the area.

"I've got to run. Talk to you later."

CHAPTER 22

Saturday 2:00 PM

Brenda turned into Jay Martin's driveway and observed a man standing next to Martin's mailbox. She got out of the car and approached the man, sizing him up as to whether he was friend or foe.

"Are you Detective Corrino?" the man asked.

"Yes. Who are you?" she answered while keeping a grip on her weapon.

"My name is Mark Alexander. I'm a friend of Jay's. He asked me to guard this mailbox until you arrived."

"Did you touch anything?"

"I opened the mailbox to see what was inside, but I didn't touch the package."

"You shouldn't have touched the damn mailbox, either." Brenda put on a pair of Latex gloves and retrieved a small yellow bubble envelope about the size of a DVD case from the mailbox.

As she headed back to her car Alexander asked, "How about giving me a ride up to the house?"

"All right. Get in. You're that photographer guy, aren't you?"

"Yes."

"When was the last time you saw Alana Andrews alive?"

"About two weeks before they found her."

"Did you photograph her?"

"Yeah, about three months ago."

"Did you photograph Cindee Cox, too?"

"Yeah, a long time ago. Probably about two years ago. Why?"

"I'll ask the questions. Did you also photograph Candie Street?"

"Candie? Yeah. I did a complete session with her last week. In fact, I'm waiting for her to call me to go over a few of the shots so I can finish putting her portfolio together."

"When's the last time you had contact with her?"

"I told you, last week."

"You haven't spoken with her on the phone or anything?"

"I'm planning on calling her Monday if I don't hear from her over the weekend."

"Do you have an exclusive or something on all the young, new, talented women in Fairfield County?"

"No. But I do get plenty of referrals from my clients, and Jay helps me out by recommending me when he signs up new talent."

She pulled into the circular driveway. The house was lit up like a birthday cake.

"Another party tonight?"

"No. Just a few friends visiting."

"Out you go."

"Would you like to come in for a drink, Detective?" he asked after he exited the car, standing there holding the door open.

"Maybe some other time when I'm off duty. Are you sure Mr.

Martin isn't having a party? I see seven or eight cars, and it looks like every light in the house is on."

"Just about every night is happening here. People just drop in, and before you know it there's a mini-party going on. Jay loves to be surrounded by people."

"Well, I guess. I don't hear a party."

"Who needs sound to have a party?"

"From what I hear he likes to party with young women."

"Who doesn't? He likes to have fun and so do they. I'd love to photograph you sometime, Detective. Have you done any modeling?"

"In my younger days."

"I knew it. I still have a pretty good eye. When was it, last year?" Alexander said, sporting a boyish grin.

Brenda grew increasingly uncomfortable talking to him. There was something about his ladies'-man attitude that really rubbed her the wrong way. *Who the fuck does he think he is flirting with me like that? I'm in charge here, not him.* "Where were you last night?"

"Last night?"

"Yeah, last night."

"I was home. Why?"

"All night?"

"Yeah. Why?"

"Were you alone?"

"Yes, alone. Now what's with all the questions?"

"Remember, I ask the questions."

"Do you have a business card on you?"

"No. Why? Are you considering a photo session?"

"Why would I need to do a photo session?"

"Because it's fun. I'd even do the session and proofs for free. If you don't purchase any photos it won't cost you anything except two hours of your time. I have a complete studio at my house and a very private pool area for outside shots. I'm in the book under Celebrity Sightings. Give me a call and maybe we can set something up."

Choosing not to address his request she told him to close the door. But he didn't, so she jerked the car away, pulling the door out of his hands, allowing it to close on its own. She left him standing there with his stupid little grin and a bulge in his pants. *Horny little bastard. He gets a hard-on talking about photographing me.* She decided to call Frank and find out his location.

"Gianni."

"Frank, it's Brenda. Looks like we might have another DVD. Are you heading back to the station?"

"Yeah. Have the guys go over the DVD for prints and DNA."

"Remember that guy Cindee Cox spent the night with?"

"Yeah. The photographer."

"Mark Alexander. I met him tonight at Martin's house. He's quite a player. I'm going to have Lois do a background check on him. I also should have a few of his fingerprints on my car. I'll have the lab lift them for future comparisons. Guess what else? He did portfolios for Alana, Candie, and Cindee Cox, too."

"I'm going to find out where Perceo was last night. I'll swing by his place and talk to him. See you in about an hour."

Brenda hung up and dialed Lois. "Lois. I want you to drop whatever you're doing and dig up everything you can on a Mark Alexander. He's Caucasian, about thirty-five years old, medium build, brown hair and eyes, and over six feet tall. He lives in the Sasco Beach area, and he runs a business called Celebrity Sightings out of a home photography studio. See if he has a business license. The license application should give us some good information. Look him up in the phone book under photographers and get his address. Check him for priors, too. I'll be there in about ten minutes."

"Okay, I'll get started."

CHAPTER 23

Frank pulled into the parking lot at Pine Creek Condominiums and immediately checked to see if the white Porsche Boxster was parked in space 2-C. The sports car was there, and it had company. A black, Mercedes four-door sedan occupied the 2-C visitor space. Frank went upstairs and headed for Perceo's unit. He put his ear to the door and could hear two men talking. Old blue eyes wasn't crooning tonight. Frank knocked on the door and got an immediate response.

"Who is it?" someone shouted from within.

"Fairfield Police, Detective Gianni."

"Come in, Detective," said Tony Perceo as he swung open the door. "You must have ESP. I was just talking about you."

"All good things, I assume," said Gianni, causing a laugh to bellow from Perceo.

A black guy was seated on the sofa wearing a midnight-blue Armani Suit, with soft, white pinstripes that resembled faded chalk lines. He stood up and put out his hand when Perceo said, "Detective Gianni, this is my friend and occasional boss, David Williams."

"So you're the PI that gets Perceo his bodyguard gigs," Frank said as he grabbed his hand firmly and shook it.

Williams laughed loudly and said, "I guess you could say that. He's not very good, though. He got fired from the first gig."

"Yeah, and the second gig ended in murder," Gianni quickly added, succeeding to create duress.

"I assure you, Detective, Tony didn't have anything to do with that. He's a retired police officer, you know."

"Yeah, I know all about his retirement from New York's finest. So Mr. Perceo says he was talking about me just before I knocked. What's that about?"

"He's hiring me to do some investigating into the Alana Andrews murder. He's concerned that you're trying to pin the murder on him."

"That's interesting." Frank turned towards Perceo and got right in his face and said, "Where were you last night?"

"I was here."

"All night?"

"Yeah."

"Can you prove it? Did anyone see you?"

"David and his girlfriend stopped over for a few drinks. What's this about?"

"You have another murder last night?"

"What makes you say that?"

"Fuck you, Gianni! Why are you playing these fucking games with us?" asked Williams as he took a step towards him. "We're both ex-cops, for Christ sake. Tell us what's going on. Maybe we can help."

"A woman named Candie Street was murdered last night and left up at Lake Mohegan. Same M.O. as Alana Andrews."

"Holy shit. You have a serial killer on your hands?" asked Perceo.

"Looks that way. Don't make any plans to leave town in the near future."

"What the hell is wrong with you, Gianni? Do I look like a fucking serial killer to you?"

"You're still a person of interest as far as I'm concerned. So unless you and Mr. Williams can tell me who the murderer is, I'm asking you not to leave town. You still got a problem with that?"

Perceo opened the door and said, "Have a good evening, Detective, and don't let the door hit you in the ass on your way out."

Frank stepped out silently as the door slammed behind him.

CHAPTER 24

Sunday 8:30 AM

The following morning Frank and Brenda began discussing the list of possible suspects, agreeing that they didn't have much.

"Frank?"

"Yeah."

"Did I tell you that asshole Alexander wants to photograph me in his studio?"

"What?"

"Can you believe that crap?"

"Typical pick-up line for a photographer, I guess."

"I don't know. Something about that guy that gives me the creeps. He photographed both victims and Cindee, too."

"Yeah, you told me. He also photographed thousands of other women that aren't dead, too."

"I've got Lois working up a background check. Just like you

know serial predators, I know men. I'm telling you, that guy is screwed up someway, somehow."

"Let's face it. You're an attractive woman. He's a single guy, so he takes a shot. Maybe he figures he'll get lucky and put another notch on the old bedpost. That doesn't make him a murderer."

"I'd like to talk to some of the other women he's photographed. Maybe they could give us some insight into his personality."

"How are you going to get the names?"

"I'll just ask him. He's cocky enough to give me some names."

"That guy Alexander is quite a character," Lois said as she approached the detectives.

"You got something?"

"Yeah. We ran the prints we lifted off your car door. From 1984 to 1997 he worked for Solutions, a large software company in California. He lost his job do to reorganization. In 1998 he was considered a suspect in the rape of a female college student. But his DNA didn't match, and when she couldn't pick him out of a lineup he was released. The case is still unsolved."

"Let me see the printout, Lois," Brenda said as she snatched it from her hand like a barracuda.

"Son of a bitch, Frank! That was a multiple rape, too. She was raped and sodomized several times over a two-day period. The bastard blindfolded her and tied her to a bed. He used dildos and vibrators on her, too. She wasn't positive, but she thought that there may have been more than one man that raped her. She had traces of Rohyphol in her system, too. There are an awful lot of similarities to our case, Frank. I'm telling you, Alexander could be our man."

"Yeah, but there weren't any piercings, and she's not dead. I wonder how he became a suspect."

"The report doesn't say. I'll give the LAPD a call tomorrow and see if I can speak to the investigating officer."

"Why not today?"

"Because it's Sunday. We may be working twenty-four/seven on this case but they probably get a day off once in a while."

"Try today, Lois," Frank said, out-ranking Brenda. "It may be his weekend to work."

Looking back at Frank, Brenda asked, "If Alexander is our guy, how does he get the body from Sasco Beach to Lake Mohegan without leaving a trail?"

"I don't know. Maybe he's not our guy."

"Ask him to send you everything he's got Lois," Brenda added without malice. "I don't want a summary. I want all the tortuous details."

"Lois," Frank said. "Since you did such a good job on Alexander, I'll give you an even easier one. Contact NYPD and see if there are any blemishes on Detective Tony Perceo's tour of duty. He retired in 2000."

"By the way, Detective, the lab said the package, plastic case, and DVD were wiped clean. The DVD was recorded with the same video camera. It's on your desk."

"Thanks, Lois. You want to look at it now, Brenda?"

"Yeah. Let's get it over with."

Frank and Brenda grabbed the DVD and went into the Media Center. Frank closed the door and the blinds. At least the police could give Candie Street a little dignity. Brenda inserted the DVD into the player and the television screen became alive with a masked naked woman, bound to the same bed that had held Alana Andrews. She had auburn hair, blue eyes, and a slender figure with large breasts. Her breasts appeared natural. Brenda didn't doubt for one second that it was Candie Street.

"Let me go," yelled Candie as a figure entered the room. As with the previous victim, he roughly grabbed her nipples one at a time and pierced them to install the gold nipple jewelry. She winced and began to sob as she lifted her head up as high as she could to see what he did to her.

"Please, don't mutilate me. I'll do anything you want. Untie me and I'll give you the best sex you ever had in your life. You want money? I can give you as much as you want."

Her words fell on deaf ears as the figure left the room and the screen went black. When the recording began again, as in Alana's recording, Candie appeared to be raped by three men.

"Do you think they are the same three men that raped Alana?" Brenda asked Frank.

"Maybe. We'll have to get the lab to play them side by side and look for comparisons. I'm sure as hell not going to do it."

"And why does the last rapist have to slap her on the ass like she's some two-bit street whore? What does it mean, Frank? Is he trying to tell us something?"

"Maybe he wants her to feel like a whore. Maybe in his eyes, she is a whore, and he wants her to know it. Maybe she put out for other guys but not for him, and this is his way of evening the score. I don't know. He and his friends are sick bastards. That much I know for sure."

Candie was then sodomized and chocked to death with the large dildos, as tears rolled down Brenda's cheeks. Frank pulled Brenda out of her chair and wrapped his arms around her, giving her a strong deep hug. He enjoyed the sweet fragrance of her perfume, and with her firm breasts pressing against his chest, he became unwillingly aroused.

"Let it out, Brenda," he whispered into her hair. "It won't leave this room. I promise you we'll get the bastard."

But Brenda didn't cry anymore as she returned Frank's embrace with a yearning that made him realize he might be crossing a line. He pulled away abruptly hoping that she didn't notice his obvious erection.

"Thanks, Frank. I really needed that. I can't believe that anyone could treat a human being like that. Like a piece of garbage. He's finished the meal, and what's left is the garbage to be disposed of."

After a minute of silence, as she dabbed her eyes with a tissue Frank asked, "Is Doctor Crowe working today?"

"Yeah."

"Why don't we go downstairs and see what he has to say about Candie Street. Maybe he found something new that we missed at the crime scene."

"You go, Frank," she said as she checked her makeup with a mirror. "I'll join you in a few minutes after I regain my composure."

"Yeah sure. Take your time. I'll ask Lois to walk the DVD back over to the lab for them to look for similarities."

CHAPTER 25

Doctor Crowe appeared to be sniffing Candie Street's vagina as Frank pushed open the door to the Medical Examiners Room. Her lifeless body lay on the stainless steel gurney with her legs placed in the stirrups. Her body was being disrespected again, but this time with good intentions. As Frank approached the body he suddenly realized that she had been cut open from her neck down to her sternum, and he had to turn away for a moment.

"She's got that same rash in the pubic area as the last victim," Darren said without looking up, as Frank approached. "I'll send some skin samples to the lab, but you can assume it's the same thing as the first victim."

"Body lice?"

"So, you were paying attention at the last autopsy."

"Actually, Brenda told me about it. Anything not the same?"

"Her breasts are real. Completely natural. I'd say they're about 38 Ds. Remember how Ms. Andrews's breasts defied gravity? Look at these. They're both flopped over to the side. The real deal."

"Anything else?"

"No. Same M.O. Raped, then sodomized, and choked to death with a ten-inch dildo."

"Semen?"

"Yeah and plenty of it. Probably multiple intercourse again."

"You said she was sodomized?"

"With the dildo. Same as Ms. Andrews."

"Let me know as soon as you get the DNA results on the semen. I'd like to know if they match the first three." Frank headed for the door.

"Yeah. Okay. Is Brenda working today?"

Frank held the door half open as he said, "Yeah. She was going to join us, but something came up."

"Tell her I was asking for her," Darren shouted as the door swung shut.

Frank started to jog up the stairs and ran right into Brenda, almost knocking her to the floor. "Sorry. You all right?"

"Yeah. I guess so. What did you find out?"

"It appears that every thing is the same as with the first victim except for her breasts. They are the real deal, as Doctor Crowe put it. No implants. She has the same rash, too."

"The real deal, huh. Are those his words?"

"Yeah."

"Lice?"

"No, just the rash."

Brenda continued towards the M.E. as Frank watched her from behind. He could never admit to anyone that he really enjoyed working with her. Nor could he admit that he really enjoyed looking at her. He reasoned to himself that he was jealous of her relationship with Doctor Crowe. He didn't understand why. His wife was beautiful, too, and he loved her very much. Yet he was compelled to watch until her wiggle as it disappeared through the door.

CHAPTER 26

"Retired detective Tony Perceo has a clean record according to the NYPD," Lois said as she caught Frank walking over towards his desk. "He attended the police academy right after college and worked his way up the ladder. He retired in two thousand after twenty years on the force at the age of forty-five from the detective division to be with his ill wife. She was an actress. They were married for twelve years. She passed away from cancer when she was only thirty-seven years old."

"No blemishes?"

"No."

"What about Alexander?"

"I spoke with the detective that handled the investigation, a Detective O'Leary. He didn't remember too many details about the case, but he's sending over a copy of the file. I asked him to overnight it."

"Good."

"By the way, Mrs. Pucho called looking for Brenda," Lois said, waving a message pad towards him as she headed for Brenda's desk. "She didn't want to use voicemail."

"Yeah," Frank said as he intercepted the pad and ripped off the top page. Instead of leaving the note by Brenda's phone he decided to return the call himself. Mrs. Pucho answered on the second ring.

"Hello."

"Mrs. Pucho?"

"Yes."

"Hi. This is Detective Corrino's partner, Detective Gianni. I was told that you called today to speak with Detective Corrino. She's busy right now. Is there anything I can help you with?"

"It's about Miss Cox. I haven't seen her for a few days. I've tried calling her and knocked on her door, but she doesn't answer. It's just like the last time. Her car hasn't left the driveway."

"Perhaps somebody picked her up or she left for a bike ride."

"I didn't see or hear any cars. Besides, after the last incident, she said she would tell me when she was going to be away for a few days so I wouldn't worry. I hope she left enough food for her cat."

"I wouldn't worry too much about it. She'll probably come home today."

"I hope you're right. Please tell Detective Corrino I called."

"Okay."

Frank called the M.E. office to talk to Brenda, but no one answered, so he headed back down there. As he opened the door he could see Brenda and Darren standing in the corner kissing and humping each other. *Wow, are they ever hot for each other.*

"Sorry to spoil the party, kids, but I need to speak to you Brenda," Frank said as Brenda pushed Darren away and straightened out her clothes.

"Shit. What's up, Frank?" Brenda asked as she felt a few drops of perspiration beginning to penetrate the front of her blouse. Looking down she realized that she was a little unbuttoned, too, and quickly folded her arms in front of her chest.

"I'm not sure. Mrs. Pucho, Cindee Cox's neighbor called looking for you. I called her back, and she thinks that Cindee Cox is missing again. She promised to tell her when she planned to be gone for a few days so that she could feed her cat. She's worried. Cox's car is still in the driveway. Maybe she went for another bike ride over to Alexander's house."

"Or maybe somebody picked her up."

"Mrs. Pucho said she didn't see or hear any cars. But let's face it; she can't be looking out the window twenty four/seven."

"You want to bet? There's really nothing we can do about it anyway, other than take a ride by her house and see if anything looks out of place."

"Why don't we give it another day? I've got a better idea. Let's pay Mark Alexander a visit and ask him if he knows where she might be. Maybe she's there. Maybe we shake him up a little."

"All right. Wait for me upstairs. I'll be up in a minute."

Looking at Darren, Frank said with a smirk, "If you're not up in five minutes I'm leaving without you."

"Will you get the fuck out of here, Frank," Brenda shouted in frustration.

Frank suppressed a laugh but couldn't help a grin as he turned and headed out the door.

CHAPTER 27

Sunday 9:00 PM

"Can I pick them this time?" Mya asked Mark as they drove towards New Haven.

"No. You know I like to use the same guys. Less risk. What's it matter to you who I get to do it?"

"You know I like to watch. I want to see guys with real big ones teach her a lesson."

"They're all horny for a prime piece of ass. How are you going to know if they have big dicks?"

"Just leave it up to me. Maybe we should get a woman, too. You know, a butch would really appreciate doing a beautiful princess like her."

"No way. We stick with the same three guys. There's the green. Let's find a place to park and look for my main man."

The New Haven Green was situated in the heart of the financial district and a block from prestigious Yale University in the city of New Haven, about twenty-six miles north of Fairfield. The Connecticut Financial Center on Church Street was the tallest office building in New Haven. Its beautiful granite structure soared high above the trees. A bank and a small restaurant were located on the first floor. The corporate offices of the local electric utility, The United Illuminating Company occupied the fourth through sixteen floors. The remaining ten floors housed the offices of federal judges and prosecutors. Right behind the Connecticut Financial Center was the Federal Building and post office where offices of the federal government were located. On the north side of the Connecticut Financial Center was New Haven City Hall, housed in a refurbished, two-story brownstone. The federal courthouse with its fancy concrete pillars was on the other side. The buildings were situated across the street from the center of the green.

"It's ironic, isn't it? All these federal assholes work right across the street from all these vagabonds," Alexander said as he slowed to check out a parking space.

On the north side of the green was Elm Street where the New Haven Public Library, State Court House, and Yale University Visitor Center resided. In between the visitor center and library was Temple Street. It actually ran through the center of the green, north and south, parallel to Church Street. Three churches on Temple Street attempted to humble all that walked past them. Temple Street led on to Chapel Street, the southern border of the green. The Chapel Square Mall with the Omni Hotel right behind it on Temple Street consumed the entire block south of the green. Heading west on Chapel one block brought you to College Street and the Shubert Theater, known for its Broadway-style shows and actors. Chapel Street consisted of a variety of clothing stores, restaurants, specialty shops, the Yale Center for British Art, the Yale Repertory Theater, and the Yale University Art Gallery.

Heading north on College brought you back to Elm Street. With all its historic buildings, city, state, and federal government, surrounding it, the New Haven Green continued to be a gathering place for many homeless people. From June to October many of them crash landed on a park bench and spent the night. They were awakened before seven in the morning by the police to disperse them out of sight before the businessmen started making their way across the green to their workplaces.

Alexander parked directly across from the federal courthouse, surrounded by the buildings of authority on Church Street.

"Let's go, Mya."

Entering the green was like entering a foreign country. As they approached the picnic tables full of people the talking would cease. Once they were out of earshot, the talking would resume. A stench of filth and booze filled the air. The homeless were mostly men. Many of them had their shopping carts loaded with their entire belongings, as well as recyclable bottles and cans that they pulled out of garbage cans. Mark was looking for a guy called Sundance. He was sort of a loner but he had some friends. He managed to survive everyday without bottles and cans or wheeling around a shopping cart.

Sundance was a cool dude with long, stringy blonde hair. His face was as weathered as an old leather shoe, and when he smiled you could notice he was missing several teeth. He was always talking to himself or anyone who cared to listen. He appeared to be in good physical condition considering the situation. He challenged Mark to an arm wrestle when they first met, but it wasn't much of a contest. Sundance made fast work of him and became somewhat of a hero amongst his homeless family. Sundance would notify the other two players.

"There he is, Mya," Mark said excitedly. But Mya wasn't there. She had wandered off and was sitting at a table consisting mostly of homeless women. He went over and pulled her off the bench. The women started yelling at Mark, but Mya assured them that nothing was wrong.

"Thanks for the information, ladies," said Mya as she began to walk away with Mark.

"God damn it, Mya. I told you no women."

"I know. There was one guy sitting there and one of them had her hand down the front of his pants and was jacking him off. I stopped to talk to her, and she didn't miss a single stroke. It was like she was doing him a favor or something. I asked her about the men who hang out here."

"I spotted Sundance over by the water fountain talking to himself. Come on. Let's see if we can get his attention."

As they approached the fountain it was obvious that most of the people hanging around there weren't homeless. Drug activity and prostitution was going on. The homeless didn't need to create new problems for themselves.

"There he is. Hey, Sundance!"

"What's up, Kodak?" he answered Mark with a fatigued smile.

"I could use your assistance again. Do you think you can talk to your friends about another little party for Tuesday night?"

Sundance took a long hard look at Mya and said, "Are you the one I'll be servicing?"

"You wish."

"Hey, be cool. She's my girlfriend. You know the identity can't be revealed. I've got a beautiful blond with a centerfold body waiting for you. She can't wait to have three strangers fulfill her fantasy. That's why she's willing to pay you guys to do it."

"Why does she have to wear that fucking mask, man?"

"I told you, it's because she doesn't want you guys to know who she is. Now do you want the job or not? I'm sure it won't be hard to replace you."

"You don't have to get pissed off, Kodak. Of course I want to fuck a beautiful woman, but I want more money, since I can't see her beautiful face. For all I know, she's a real ugly bitch."

"What? Are you kidding me? You should be paying her for the privilege. I'll tell you what. Since you help me by getting the other two guys, I'll tell her that we have to pay you a bonus. I assume that you guys have kept your mouths shut about this arrangement."

"I know I have. I can only get one other guy this time. Is that okay?"

"Fuck no! It has to be three."

"I haven't seen Roberto at all this week. He must have gone to live with his daughter in Boston. He was always saying that some day his daughter would figure out that he lived on the street and she'd make him go live with her. I figured it was just bullshit, but maybe that's where he went."

"I've got an idea," Mya said.

"I told you no women."

"I know. Hey, Sundance. Do you know a guy named Hound Dog?"

"Yeah. He's a big dude. I think he used to be a wrestler or something. Why?"

"I was told by some of those ladies over there that he has a super big cock. Our centerfold likes big dicks. Do you think he'd be willing to help us out?"

"I don't see why not."

"Can we trust him to keep his mouth shut?" asked Mark. "These women that hire me to pay you want their privacy respected."

"Stay here while I look for him."

Mark and Mya sat down on the concrete circular bench that surrounded the fountain. "That Sundance is something else," Mya said.

"Yeah. He's no dummy either. When I went to school here we got to know some of these homeless guys. Some of these people are college graduates. How's that for a fucking wake-up call?"

"No shit! But I thought you went to college in California?"

"That was for my undergraduate in Art and Photography? When my aunt died and I inherited the Connecticut properties, I moved here and got my MBA from Yale."

"Here he comes."

Walking alongside Sundance was a big black dude with a shaved head and dragon tattoos up and down both arms. He was over six feet tall and built like a football player. He offered them a toothless smile as he got closer.

"This is Hound Dog," Sundance proudly announced.

"Are you the pretty lady that wants me to fuck her?" Hound Dog asked Mya as he approached them.

"You wish. Actually, she's way hotter than I am. You won't be disappointed. Are you the guy with the extra large equipment?"

"Who told you that?" asked Hound Dog, his malodorous breath forcing her to stop breathing and take a step backward to avoid the stench.

"One of the women over there," she said pointing towards the table that she visited earlier.

Hound Dog laughed loudly before saying, "She says she's a therapeutic nurse. I bet she will handle all the guys here sooner or later and half the women, too. She's one horny control-freak bitch."

"Did Sundance tell you the rules?" Alexander asked Hound Dog. He was obviously tired of the bullshit.

"Yeah. She's a rich bitch that wants to fulfill a gang-bang fantasy. No questions, no talking to anyone, including the bitch, right?"

"Right. If you do a good job and keep your mouth shut, I'll use you again. If you don't keep your trap shut I'll have to kill you. Understand?"

"Kill me? Who the fuck do you think you are? I'll kill you."

"Have you seen Roberto lately?" Mark said as if Hound Dog hadn't spoken.

"No. I heard he's staying with his daughter in Boston."

"You sure about that? Maybe he's dead. "Maybe he couldn't keep his mouth shut. I get paid a lot of money to arrange these get-togethers. I've got a good thing going with these women. Do you want in or not? I'm sure I can find someone else to do it. It's not everyday that a centerfold wants you to fuck her, is it? All you have to do is keep your mouth shut. Look at Sundance. This will be his third time in less than two weeks. He knows he has a good thing going here."

"Tuesday night?"

"Yeah. Two nights from tonight. I'll pick the three of you up at nine and have you back here by midnight. Wait for me at the fountain."

"Do you think you can drop me off a few blocks from here instead?" asked Hound Dog.

"No problem. See you guys tomorrow. Sundance, don't forget to tell your buddy, Stan."

"No problem. He'll be here."

Back in the car Mark asked, "Would you like to stop for a drink? I'm feeling super horny right now."

"I can't. I told you I have to see David tonight."

"Why are you still going out with that loser?"

"He's not such a bad guy. Besides he helps me with some of my criminal cases. He still has some connections with the police and the courts. Investigative work doesn't come cheap you know."

"You have to sleep with him don't you?"

"Yeah, but it's business. Did you really kill that Roberto guy?"

"No. I just wanted to scare those assholes."

CHAPTER 28

Sunday 11:30 PM

David Williams was already waiting in the parking lot of the Paradise Club, a popular strip joint over on the west side of town in nearby Stamford, when Mya showed up. While he waited he reminisced about how Mya worked her way through law school as a stripper. They officially met when he was doing P.I. work for a celebrity, and Mya called him as a witness in the case. He recognized her immediately as one of the strippers from the club, even though he never saw her with clothes on before that day. She knew him as a polite patron who loved to stuff dollar bills in her panties and didn't allow his fingers to wander. During the trial, neither one let on that they knew each other from the club.

David was still an impressive figure for a fifty-three-year-old former cop. He retired from the New York City Police Department, detective division after twenty-five years of service. He began GOTTCHA, a private investigation business specializing in infidelities. He did a lot of work for celebrities. At five foot eleven and two hundred pounds he could still rough it up when he had to.

David's ten year marriage ended in divorce in 1990.

Mya spotted his black Mercedes as soon as she pulled into the parking lot and pulled up alongside it. She didn't like returning to the Paradise Club. Now that she was an attorney and had a respectable career she didn't want to be reminded of her seedy past of stripping, lap dancing, and when the price was right, or the rent was due, sex acts.

"Hey, sugar," she said lowering her window as she drove up alongside of him.

"Why don't you park it, and we'll go in and have a drink."

"You know I don't like going in there." Why don't we go back to your place and have that drink?"

"You know I enjoy watching the young dancers."

"I'll strip for you, David. It'll be like old times. Besides, I'm probably younger than at least half of them. Remember Nora Jean with the blonde wig? Shit, she had to be forty."

David laughed low and deep as the vision of the Monroe wannabe danced in his head. "The only thing that saved her job was her tits. They always looked good because of the silicone."

"Yeah, and the fact that she was the cheapest blowjob in the club didn't hurt either."

"Okay, you win. I'm aroused. Follow me over to my place."

*

Monday, April 26, 2004 12:10 AM

The Audi was parked in the driveway when Brenda and Frank arrived at Alexander's.

"Would you look at this freaking place, Frank," Brenda whispered. "How the hell can he afford the upkeep?"

"Yeah. I guess it must really pay well to photograph the rich and famous." Frank touched the hood and said, "It's still warm. I wonder where our boy has been."

The huge brick mansion was built in the early nineteen hundreds and was a stone's throw from the Country Club of Fairfield. The house had twenty-four rooms, including ten bedrooms, eight bathrooms, and six fireplaces. It sat back six hundred feet from Sasco Hill Road on ten level acres, affording Alexander plenty of privacy. An unattached, four-car garage was in front of the house and to the left, so that you couldn't see the end of the house from the road. Above the garage was the old servants' quarters that had been updated into a fancy guest apartment.

Alexander answered the door with a towel wrapped around his waist, his hair and muscular chest wet. "Detective Corrino, what a pleasant surprise. I hope you're not here for your photo session. I don't work this late."

"This is my partner, Detective Gianni," she said while completely ignoring his arrogant remark. "We'd like to ask you a few questions."

"Why must you be so formal? Come in and sit down while I get dressed. You caught me in the shower."

While he was gone they snooped around a little, examining photographs, paintings, and artifacts that could only be described as priceless heirlooms. Brenda wandered into the kitchen and was surprised to see dirty glasses everywhere.

Alexander strolled back into the room saying, "See anything you like?" After no response he said, "So what can I do for the Fairfield P.D?"

"Where were you tonight?" asked Frank.

"I was out with a girlfriend."

"Have you seen Cindee Cox recently?" asked Brenda.

"No. Why?"

"She may be missing."

"Missing? For how long?"

"Two or three days."

"She probably went on vacation."

"You live here alone?" asked Frank.

"Yeah, but I'm never lonely. My girlfriend stays over a lot. And then there are surprise guests like Cindee once in a while."

"Your girlfriend doesn't mind?" Brenda asked.

"Not at all. We both date other people."

"What's her name?"

"Mya Bates. She's an attorney."

"We'd like to look around, do you mind?"

"Do you have a warrant or something?"

"No, but we can get one," Brenda said.

"Then I suggest you do that. I don't have anything to hide, but what's right is right. Go get your warrant and then you can look all you want." He walked quickly to the door and yanked it open. They took the hint and left without another word.

When they got back into the car Frank said, "You look like the cat the swallowed the canary. What's up?"

"These," Brenda said as she pulled out a book of matches from her pocket and a dirty crystal goblet from under her leather jacket. "I'm going to have the lab check the residue for Rohyphol. The matches are from a place called the Pleasure Chest. Ever hear of it?"

"No."

"Maybe the victims hung out there."

"You know we can't use any of that stuff as evidence."

"I know, but if the glass does test positive for Rohyphol there's a good chance that he's our man, and maybe the lieutenant will authorize a surveillance team."

*

Alexander watched them drive away until their taillights disappeared past the country club and up Sasco Hill Road, before returning to his bedroom and a comatose Cindee Cox. He stared at her beautiful naked body, fighting off an urge to do her one last time. He had his way with her for the past two days, but still wanted more. There wasn't time for that now. *I can't take the chance that they'll return with a search warrant. I have to move her to Easton now.* "Oh, what the hell. The night is young," he whispered in her ear as he took off his clothes and lay on the bed beside her, cupping her breasts with his hands. "You want to do it again, don't you, Cindee? I thought so," he said when she didn't respond. "That's okay. I'll do all the work this time. You just lay there and enjoy it. When we're finished, I'll get you cleaned up for our jaunt to the lake."

CHAPTER 29

Brenda and Frank both arrived early on Monday morning in spite of getting home late last night. They were driven by the fact that time might be running out for Cindee Cox. Brenda went down to the lab with the goblet and matchbook before going up to her desk.

"I'm surprised to see you here so early," Frank said as Brenda came into view.

"That's what I was going to say when I saw you. I dropped off the matchbook and goblet at the lab. They promised they would call me with some preliminary results within two or three hours."

"Frank...Brenda. My office. Now!"

"What's up, Lieutenant?" asked Frank.

"The police commissioner's office got a call this morning from Mark Alexander complaining about police harassment. He said you two went calling after midnight demanding to search his house without a warrant."

"I asked him if he would mind us looking around, and he said not without a warrant," Brenda injected. "So we left."

"You shouldn't be doing shit like that. You know better," the lieutenant said, turning his attention to Frank. "Do you have anything worthwhile on these murders yet?"

"Mark Alexander was considered a suspect for a similar crime in California in 1998. A student was raped several times over a two-day period. She even had traces of Rohypnol in her system. She was blindfolded, so she couldn't ID him. His DNA didn't match up, and they released him. The case is still unsolved."

"Those date rape drugs are popular in California. I find it interestingly coincidental. Do you have any other suspects?"

"We are looking at two other guys, but," Frank stopped, wishing he hadn't started the sentence.

"But what?"

"They're both retired detectives from the N.Y.P.D."

"Jesus H. Christ. That's all I need. You're going after retired cops. Were they suspected of some wrong doings during their careers?"

"No."

"Then why, Frank? Are you fucking crazy or something? Maybe you're having trouble at home and you can't think straight. Is that it?"

When he didn't answer the lieutenant said, "I'm really disappointed with you, Frank. It's been a week. We have two dead bodies and the best you can do is a photographer and two retired cops with exemplary records. I've got the first selectman breathing down my neck for an arrest. He wants us to call in the Feds. If we don't, he will. I don't know if I can stop him. He's getting a lot of pressure from the *Connecticut Post* and Channel Eight. They keep sending reporters down here looking for answers. We are probably going to have to schedule a press conference real soon and give them something. So get the hell out of my office and find the murderer before the first selectman calls the FBI, and the captain puts the last nail in my coffin."

"Lieutenant., I might need a surveillance team tomorrow," Brenda said.

"A surveillance team for who?"

"Alexander."

Brenda could see that Lieutenant Nelson was about to bite her head off. "I borrowed a dirty goblet from Alexander's kitchen, and I'm having the lab check it for Rohypnol. If it tests positive I'd like to keep an eye on him until Cindee Cox is located."

"You what? You took it without a warrant? You know that's inadmissible. Frank, what the hell are you teaching her?"

Before Frank could answer, Brenda continued, "He's not teaching me anything. I mean, of course I know it's inadmissible. He didn't know I took it until we were out of the house. I just wanted to know if we should keep looking at this guy. If it tests positive, maybe we could get a search warrant and obtain some legal evidence."

"You're not going to get a judge to give you a search warrant based on illegally obtained evidence. Come on, Corrino. I know you're smarter than that. Now will you get the fuck out of my office before I throw you out?"

"Is that a yes or a no to the surveillance team, Lieu?" asked Brenda as she and Frank headed for the door.

Lieutenant Nelson's stare would have been answer enough for most cops, but Brenda wasn't going to back down. She complemented his stare with her own, as she waited for an answer. Frank slipped out the door, not wanting to get in the middle of it. Before the lieutenant could speak she said, "Why the hell did you accept me into homicide? If you don't like the way I operate demote me. All I know is that we have two unsolved murders and a possible third one if we don't find Cindee Cox. The first selectman is breathing down our necks, and the captain wants your ass on a silver platter. Unless you have some better ideas, I'm going to need that surveillance team tomorrow."

"Are you sure you're a woman, Corrino?"

"What?"

"You've got a huge set of balls for a woman. Come see me after you get something from the lab, and we'll discuss it again."

"Thanks, Lieutenant," Brenda said with a cautious smile as she left the office.

"Don't be thanking me yet."

"You all right?" Frank asked her as she walked back towards him.

"Couldn't be better."

"I got a call from a buddy of mine who's with the New Haven P.D. He said a resident homeless guy was recently murdered. He was strangled with a rope."

"So."

"I was discussing our case with him a few days ago, and he remembered that I said the rapist might have lice. This dead guy had lice. Not only that, but it sounds like he was strangled with the same type rope that was used to tie our victims to the tree and bed. I'm meeting up with him for lunch, and he said he would bring me in to look at the rope and preliminary reports."

"No shit! When was he murdered?"

"They found him Saturday night. They estimated the time of death to be about one o'clock Saturday morning."

"That's the same day that we found Candie Street. You think the murderer is a homeless person?"

"Or maybe this guy knew too much and was shooting off his mouth, so the murderer shut him up permanently. Anyway, I'm going to take a ride to New Haven and check it out."

"All right. I'll hang here for a while and see what the lab turns up.

*

Brenda decided to satisfy her curiosity and check out the Pleasure Chest on the Internet from the Media room. She ran a Google search and found it in about two seconds at www.pleasurechest.com. The website wasn't too flashy nor did nudity or erotica take center stage. The first thing Brenda did was click on the *Directions* tab.

The Pleasure Chest is located on ten acres in the quaint town of Vista, New York, just a stone's throw over the Connecticut border. Its remote location adds to the mystique and intrigue of both members and visitors alike. We have his and hers locker rooms with towels and showers. Every locker has an oriental, designer-silk robe and two towels. The Foreplay Lounge serves wine, beer, and soda and has a 54" wide screen television continually showing explicit adult movies. The main attraction is the Roman Empire room. It is the size of a football field, and it's where all the serious activities commence. There are no overnight accommodations at the Pleasure Chest, however there are many motels within a few miles if you wish to continue your party after we close. The parking area is large enough to accommodate your RV; however there are no facilities for hookups. We are open from 7:00 PM-3:00 AM, Monday-Saturday. We do not post directions nor our address on this website to discourage the curious. After you and your partner have completed the phone interview and make a reservation, you will be given directions. All reservations require a credit card. Call 800-FUN-TIME for more information.

Next she clicked on the *Visitors* tab.

The club offers a very open atmosphere of sexuality. You can expect to see full nudity as well as sexual activity almost anywhere in the club. Each couple is free to become as involved as they wish. It is a very low-pressure atmosphere and ideal for couples just beginning their adventures into the lifestyle. The Pleasure Chest is like any social function you might attend. We've all been to a party where we didn't know some of the guests. If you choose to roam around and watch, that's exactly what you can do all night if you like. If others ask to sit with you, remember that it does not constitute a commitment to anything else other than sharing your space, unless of course, you decide to go further. Remember that everyone you see at the club was new there once, just like you. The sooner you speak to other couples, the sooner you will get to know people, and the sooner they will get to know you. If you feel shy or awkward about just walking up to someone you'd like to meet, the staff is always happy to make introductions among couples at the parties.

What about the possibility of meeting co-workers or other people you know? This does happen but remember, we are all here for the same reason. Everyone you meet values their confidentiality as much as you do. We've seen this happen, but while it was uncomfortable at first, it always provides a good laugh later, and we have always seen them back enjoying the club again.

We are having our semi-annual Costume Theme Event on Monday, April 26. Your costume can hide your identity and reveal as little or as much as you desire. It's a chance to live your fantasy anonymously. The Costume Theme Event is the most popular event for anyone wishing to experience the life incognito. SINGLE MALES ARE NEVER WELCOME at the Pleasure Chest.

Couples and single females are always welcome. The fun begins at 7:00 PM, so call early and make your reservation. Call 800-FUN-TIME for more information.

She tried the *Members* tab, but it immediately requested a membership number and password. The *Photo Gallery* tab was her next choice. It contained about thirty photographs primarily showing off the décor and layout of the Pleasure Chest. No naked people or any people for that matter, just the locker room and showers, the Foreplay Lounge, and the bulk of the photographs were of the Roman Empire. The photos showed a huge room with many ceiling fans and plants everywhere, including what appeared to live trees that reached the ceiling. The walls were tiled on the lower half and many mirrors, paintings and photographs of nature adorned the upper half. Along the walls were cubicles filled with chairs, sofas, and mattresses. Three huge Jacuzzis, one in the middle of the room and one on each end were full of bubbling water but no people. They were large enough for twenty or thirty people. On the floor were many king size mattresses laid next to each other. The Photo Gallery did have a tab titled Adam and Eve. Brenda clicked on it and discovered two photographs of naked men and women standing side by side. One was taken from the rear and the other from the front, with their hands in front of their faces to hide their identities. *All shapes and sizes, that's for sure.*

A *Message Board* tab was available for people to write and contact each other. Many people posted photographs of themselves in various degrees of undress. Some were shown performing explicit sex acts and asking for people to write them if they like what they see. A *Classified Ads* section where singles and couples could post photos of themselves, list their vital statistics, and solicit others to meet them for drinks and more, was another feature of the website. The photos ranged from fully clothed to totally naked, and from no sexual contact to you name it. Brenda looked in both sections for a while, hoping to catch a photo of Alexander somewhere, but she had no such luck. So she logged off and did something totally unexpected. She snatched her cell phone from her purse and called 1-800—FUN-TIME. Luckily if a female called they can wave interviewing the male.

She reserved two lockers for the Monday night costume party.

The next phone call was to Darren. "Medical Examiner's Office," Darren said as he answered the phone.

"Hi, Darren, it's Brenda."

"Hey, there, Detective, what's up?"

"I need a favor."

"Sure. Anything for you?"

"I have to go undercover tonight, to a club, and I need a male escort. I kind of remember you saying that you were on days this week."

"What time, and what do I have to wear? Do I have to dress up or can I go casual?"

"Oh, it's definitely casual. Just come over to my place about six and bring a clean lab jacket."

"A lab jacket? You did say it was a club didn't you?"

"No more questions. I think you'll have fun, and you'll help me out with my case. I really need you with me. I'm afraid to go alone."

"What about Gianni? Why can't he go?"

"He's busy looking into other leads. Look, can I count on you or not?"

"Yeah. I'll see you at six."

"Don't forget the lab jacket. It's very important. Bye."

CHAPTER 30

Monday 6:00 PM

"What the hell?" Darren said when Brenda opened the door. "Why are you wearing that?"

"Don't you like it?" Brenda said as she turned around and walked back into the house, revealing that her mock nurse uniform was open in the back from the waist down, exposing her rear and a white thong.

"Are we playing doctor and naughty nurse tonight?" he said, playfully reaching for her butt.

"Yes, but let me explain."

Brenda told him about the Pleasure Chest and why she wanted to go there.

"You really think you'll see Alexander there?"

"I don't know."

"Even if you do, all it proves is that he's a swinger, not a murderer."

"Look. I just want to see how this guy acts when he's not being questioned by the police. I need to see him in his element. In other words, I need to know if this guy is as big an asshole as he seems to be. Besides, it'll be fun. Like watching a real live porno movie up close and personal."

"What am I supposed to wear? I hope you have masks for us. All we need to do is be recognized by someone, and our careers are over."

"Don't worry. I have a nice conservative costume for you," Brenda said as she handed him a white thong and matching eye mask.

"That's conservative? No way. I can't wear that."

"All right then, you can wear these white boxer shorts over the thong," Brenda said with a laugh. "I didn't think you would parade around in a thong amongst strangers. Do you think you can wear the lab coat without a shirt? If you don't show some skin people will be staring at you for the wrong reasons. Oh, I also picked you up a pair of white shower shoes, too. Get changed while I apply the finishing touches to my outfit."

Darren stripped off his clothes and pulled on the thong. He had never worn thong underwear before and couldn't help but notice how the pouch made his equipment look larger. Just the mere fact of wearing them made him horny and aroused. He slipped on the silk boxer shorts, shower shoes, and lab coat. He checked himself out in the mirror and liked what he saw. He added the mask and concluded that he wasn't recognizable.

"Looking good!" Brenda said as she entered the room sporting a long blonde wig topped off by a satin nurse's cap. "So what do you think?"

"I think we should stay home and let the doctor operate."

"Look, I can't do this alone. I'll tell you what I'll do. After we observe Alexander, we can come back here and I'll show you how appreciative this naughty nurse can be."

"I was only like half kidding. Let's take the bottle of Jack Daniels with us. I may need to drink a couple of shots to grow balls big enough to go through with it."

"Good idea."

*

It took them a little more than an hour to get to Vista, NY. Most of the trip was via Route 15. They actually exited the highway while still in Connecticut, and then the directions led them through a series of rural back roads, making them wonder if they might have taken a wrong turn along the way. Then without warning they saw a small sign that read; *Pleasure Chest— A Private Club for Members and Their Guests.*

Darren turned onto the dirt road next to the sign and Brenda said, "Wait. What the hell am I doing? I shouldn't be doing something this bizarre without Frank knowing about it."

"It's your call."

"If I call Frank, he'll have a shit fit and tell me to get the hell away from here. Let's wait in the parking lot and observe some of the people arriving. Then I'll decide about going inside."

They put on their masks drove up the dirt road that eventually became a paved road about one hundred feet from a guard shack. They both had spring jackets on for both warmth and to conceal their costumes. The man in the guard shack wore a security company uniform.

"Names?"

"Mr. and Mrs. Davison," Brenda said.

The security guard carefully looked over the list until he found their name. He asked for a credit card and swiped it. He gave it back to Brenda to sign and didn't even mention that the credit card did not say Davison. He gave them keys with locker assignments and two beverage vouchers for the Foreplay Lounge. He also handed them a pen and clipboard with a privacy form attached. "You'll both have to sign this form. It's for the protection of our members and our guests. Basically it states that you will not reveal the identity of anyone in attendance to anyone outside of the club. If you do you can expect to be sued by that person and the club, too. If you don't want to sign it you'll have to leave now, and remember no refunds."

"Have a great evening," the guard said as they returned the signed form and clip board to him. They drove up to the parking lot and found a space that gave them a good view of the entrance door. Brenda parked the car and they both slouched down in their seats.

Several men and women arrived and went inside. They surmised that most of the people were members because their stops at the security check point were brief compared to theirs. Many people wore jackets over their costumes, although some did not. By eight-thirty they did not see anyone that they knew and decided it was time for the shots of Jack. They took turns tipping the bottle until they both had a buzz.

Brenda screwed down the bottle cap and placed the bottle under the seat. She pulled Darren towards her and planted a long, sensuous kiss on his lips. "Thanks," she added as she broke away.

"Let's go in, before we change our minds," Darren said as he opened the car door.

Based on the people waiting to get checked in by two well-built men wearing bowtie g-strings, it was obvious that nurse, hooker, and harem outfits would be in abundance. Brenda and Darren took notice that their nipples were pierced with Pleasure Chest logo jewelry. The word, "Welcum," written just above the g-strings with lipstick almost caused Darren to laugh out loud, but he held it to a smile when he caught Brenda's eye. Each man stood below a sign, "Members" written on one and "Guests" on the other. They waited in the guest line behind three women that were all dressed as harem girls and a man who was supposed to be their king. Brenda tried to flirt a little with the security man as he checked her locker pass, but he was all business. He asked for their drink vouchers and replaced them with blue plastic bracelets that each had two beads. He explained that it meant they could have two drinks each in the Foreplay Lounge, elaborating that they didn't encourage excessive drinking. They could, however, purchase additional drinks by showing their locker keys and they would be charged against the credit card they have on file from their reservation. Then he directed them towards a glass door that had "Locker Rooms" stenciled on it, explaining that there were separate rooms for men and women inside.

Brenda and Darren entered their respective locker rooms, vowing to meet in the lounge in ten minutes. Brenda placed her jacket in the locker and looked around to see if she recognized anyone. Brenda adjusted her outfit, making sure that the underwire padded cups were doing their job and that her thong was straight. As she looked at herself in the mirror she checked out the harem sisters gathered behind her. She guessed they had to be in their late forties or early fifties and could still hold their own. They each wore identical sheer pink and purple mini dresses, purple thongs and silver eye masks. *Maybe they're sisters.*

"Hi. Have you been here before?" asked one of the harem girls.

Brenda turned to face her. "No. This is my first time."

"I love your outfit. Was that guy your husband?"

"No. He's my boyfriend, and it's his first time, too."

"He's cute. If you feel like sharing, send him my way," said one of harem women.

"That's up to him, but I don't think he'll be interested. We're just curious about the lifestyle and thought this was a great way to check it out. Besides, I just want him to get super horny so when I get him home he'll have plenty to give me."

The harem broke out in laughter and gave Brenda knowing glances. "What about you?" asked one of the others. "Are you looking to hook up with another guy or perhaps a woman?"

"I'm leaving my options open, but I've never been with a woman," Brenda said seductively. "Maybe I'll find out tonight," she said as she sashayed through the door marked Foreplay Lounge.

Darren was already at the bar drinking a glass of merlot and talking to a woman who was wearing a pair of running shorts. The number sixty-nine was stenciled on her bare back in large block numbers. In smaller print was written, "N Y Marathon Survivor."

"Cute outfit," Brenda said as she approached them.

"Thanks. I like yours, too. I'm Rhaine."

"I'm Brenda. Thanks for keeping Darren company. Perhaps we'll see you later," she said as she slithered between them, feeling Rhaine's nipples rake across her back.

"Gee whiz," said Rhaine. "Don't get your panties in a twist. We were just talking."

"I'm sorry," Brenda said realizing that she was acting too uptight for a place like this. "This is our first visit, and I'm nervous. Please join us for a drink."

"If you ask me to have a drink with you guys, that means we should share some foreplay until our glasses are empty or one of us decides to go into the Roman Empire."

"Really?"

"Yeah. I'm a member, and that's one of our ice breaker rules."

"Cool. I'm game if you are, Darren," Brenda said nervously while noticing for the first time that the woman had the number six on her right breast and a nine on the other.

"Why not?" answered Darren, trying not to act unnerved by the proposition.

"In that case, I'll have a glass of Pino," Rhaine said as she placed her hand on Darren's crotch, causing him to shift a bit.

"Two merlots and a glass of Pino please," Brenda said when the bartender approached. She slid her hand down Darren's backside and played with his thong, causing him to slightly flinch. Not to be out done by the ladies, he in turn put his hand on Brenda's ass and gently snapped her thong against her cheeks.

"So, is it as wild as I've heard?" asked Brenda.

"That depends on what you've heard, I guess."

"Well, you know. Everybody is screwing anybody right out in the open."

"Well, that happens all the time in the open floor area. Plenty of threesomes and foursomes happen in separate cubicles, too. The partitions give people a sense of privacy but the walls are only four feet high, and of course with open doorways. Some people hang their towels or robes across the entrance to discourage others from joining in. There are also three Jacuzzis but only foreplay is allowed in the water for health reasons. Are you two planning on spreading your wings?" Rhaine asked as she placed her other hand on Brenda's breast and gave her a kiss on the cheek.

Brenda held her ground and said," I really don't know. I'm not sure if I'm ready for a woman, if that's what you mean."

Rhaine pulled Brenda's breasts up to force her nipples to stick out from the top of her bra. Then she lowered her head and gave a nipple a friendly lick. Again Brenda held her ground.

"Now that wasn't so bad, was it?"

"No. It was nice actually."

Rhaine led Brenda's free hand to her breast and asked her to play with her nipple. Brenda did as requested.

"Now that's really turning him on," cooed Rhaine as she looked into Darren's eyes. "He just outgrew my hand!"

All three laughed as Darren finally got up his nerve and began to play with Rhaine's free breast. She closed her eyes and enjoyed the moment. When they stopped she opened her eyes and quickly finished her wine. She placed her hands over theirs and gave them a squeeze.

"Thanks for warming me up. I'm ready for some real action now. Why don't you join me?"

"Maybe later," said Brenda. "I'm not ready yet."

"Okay. I'll see you later."

With that she pushed open the door to the Roman Empire and disappeared. Brenda noticed the harem sisters sitting at the bar, looking at her with big smiles of approval. She smiled back, realizing that they must have watched their interaction with Rhaine.

Brenda grabbed Darren's penis and said, "Damn you, Darren. You're still rock hard! You can't go walking around in there looking like that."

"What the hell do you expect? Look around. Guys are getting freaking blowjobs at the other end of the bar."

"There are?" she said as she turned to look around. One of the harem women had her mouth on the king's woody. "Shit. Imagine what's going on inside."

"Well, what do you want to do? Wait here for your boy to show up? Maybe he's already inside. Or maybe he's not coming here tonight."

"Oh, he'll be here. It's the perfect opportunity for a bastard like him to nail a new piece of ass and perhaps befriend his next victim. Let's go in there and look around. Promise me you won't leave my side no matter what happens."

"I promise."

*

The scene in the Roman Empire was surreal as Brenda and Darren looked around. Naked and semi-naked people were everywhere, and plenty of them were having sex. Many others seemed to just enjoy watching. About a third wore masks. Brenda surmised that those who wore masks were probably guests. The members who pretty much knew each other literally had nothing to hide.

"Maybe we better walk around a little," Darren said as he took Brenda's hand. "We can't just stand in one spot and stare."

"Yeah, you're right. Let's head towards that Jacuzzi on the other side." They walked along a pathway that ran between wall-to-wall mattresses, observing enough sex to make you not need any for several years. As they walked they observed groups of three, four, five, six, seven, eight or more people engaged in various degrees of sex. They were relieved to reach the Jacuzzi where the sexual activity was minimal.

"Maybe we should get in the water," said Darren. "Then we could get a good look around without being noticed."

"No way am I going in that water, and neither are you. What the hell are you thinking? You are a real doctor aren't you?"

"Who can think in a place like this? Let's walk over there than and see what's going on," Darren said pointing to a crowd of about twenty people standing around a cubicle.

They were able to get close enough to recognize Alexander having intercourse with a brunette. She was telling him she'd had enough. He lifted her off her feet while continuing to penetrate her and bounced her up and down. He kissed her passionately on the lips and gave her a playful slap on the ass before he lifted her off him. She lay back down on her back and looked completely exhausted.

Alexander was completely naked and sporting a good, thick eight inches of marble-hard penis. He had a muscular build that suggested a person who worked out on a regular basis.

"Who's next?" he asked as he surveyed the onlookers. A petite redhead said she'd give it a try. "Honey, you're not much bigger than this," he said pointing to his erection. "Remember," he said to the woman. "If you can finish me off, I'll be your slave for the rest of the night."

"That's a deal, but I'm on top. I'll have you drained in no time."

"Fine with me," he said as he lay on his back and beckoned her to begin. While he waited for her to take off her gypsy costume he said to Brenda, "Hey, nurse. I may need your help if she's as good as she claims."

Brenda replied, "If she's as good as she said, you won't be any good to me or anyone else tonight."

The group of onlookers laughed at Brenda's remark and Alexander smiled. The skinny redhead had endless energy as she rode him, occasionally lifting her legs up and spinning around, causing him to moan loudly. Sometimes she would end up facing his feet, beckoning the crowd to support her efforts. After about a half hour he couldn't hold back anymore and matched her thrusts, until he was spent. She got off him and sat right on his face saying, "Okay slave, it's time for you to obey my wishes."

He easily pushed her off and said, "Will you give me a break and let me catch my breath?" while wiping the liquid that dripped from her off his face with a towel.

"That's okay. I'm too tired to enjoy it right now anyway. I'll take a rain check. Maybe we can get together later?"

"That's a date, sweetie. Look for me in an hour or so."

As he left the cubicle he walked up to Brenda and tried to put his arms around her, but she was able to sidestep him. "Are you sure you can't provide me with some first aid, Miss Nurse?" he said as he looked deep into her eyes and placed one hand on her ass and the other on his spent manhood, waving it towards her. "I could use a little tender loving care."

She wanted to slap his face but thought better of it and gave him a playful but hard slap on the ass instead. "I think you're finished for the night, sir."

"Maybe. Maybe not. That was no ordinary screw. That girl has talent. I bet you have talent. Give me a few hours to recover, and maybe you and I can get together for a screen test."

"I don't think so. I don't like a man that I can't control." Brenda grabbed Darren's hand and led him towards the Foreplay Lounge saying softly into his ear, "Let's get the hell out of here."

"Hey. Where are you going, Miss Nurse?"

His words went unanswered as Brenda and Darren disappeared through the door.

CHAPTER 31

Tuesday 7:00 AM

Darren spent the night at Brenda's. She told him that the asshole that wanted her was none other than Mark Alexander himself. She was disgusted by him and lost all desire for making love with Darren. They held each other all night instead as they lay in her bed, both exhausted from the anxiety of the evening.

In the morning he made breakfast, planning to avoid the subject entirely but Brenda had other ideas. "Darren, about last night. I want to apologize for putting you through that. I had no right. I thought it would be kind of fun and sexy. It was almost more than I could handle. I guess it proved that he really is an asshole and a horny bastard with a big dick. Does that make him a rapist and a murderer? I'll make it up to you. Can I cook you dinner tonight?"

"No. I don't think so. Maybe some other time. I want you to

concentrate on this case and solve it. Maybe Alexander is your guy and maybe he isn't. But, I suspect that he could be your man."

"What makes you say that?"

"His pompous attitude for one thing. He thinks he's God's gift to women and could have his way with any of them just for the asking. When you turned him down it really bothered him. I could tell by his body language. You embarrassed him, and he didn't like it. Did you see him slap that woman's ass when she quit and he won?"

"You know what? That happens on the DVD, too."

Brenda finished her breakfast and said, "Why don't you join me in the shower?"

"Didn't you hear a word I said?"

She got up and kissed him long and hard, pressing her body against him. "Shut up and follow me into the shower."

*

Tuesday 9:30 AM

"Where the hell you been?" asked Frank as Brenda made her way over to her desk. "I've been calling your cell phone since eight o'clock last night and it kept kicking me into your voicemail where I left you several messages."

"Sorry, Frank. I turned it off for a while and I guess I forgot to turn it back on. How did you make out in New Haven?"

"The victim definitely has lice. My buddy took me around to a few areas where the homeless hang out during the day and we asked if anybody knew the guy, and a few people did. They said he'd been bragging lately about having sex with a beautiful woman. When questioned he would say that she told him not to tell anybody anything about her. The word on the street was that he left town and went to live with his daughter in Boston."

"So maybe he was one of the three. Anyone else bragging about have sex with a beautiful woman?"

"No. He was the only one. The New Haven P.D. is going to get the word out on the street for anyone to come forward with information about guys talking about having sex with beautiful women. Maybe we'll get lucky."

"What about guys saying they have lice?"

"That's a tough one. Homeless people have pride, too."

"Detectives, I was told to bring this report up to you right away."

"And you are who?"

"He's Mike Francis, student lab boy. "He finds murder to be fascinating," said Brenda with a bit of a flirtatious tone.

"Come on, Detective Corrino. I didn't mean it like that."

"Whatever. Thanks for the report."

She ripped it open and began to read it out loud. "The residue in the glass is Rohypnol but only Alexander's fingerprints were on it. The book of matches had two sets of prints, one set being his. Do you think we could get a warrant based on this report?"

"You heard the lieutenant yesterday. You can't use illegally obtained evidence to get a warrant. Hell. He won't give you a surveillance team either."

"He will now. Otherwise, I'll do it myself."

*

It took Brenda only a few minutes to convince the lieutenant that setting up surveillance on Alexander was the right thing to do based on the lab report. He told her to tell Frank and no one else.

The plan was for Brenda and Frank to pay Alexander a visit to verify that he was still home. An unmarked car parked in the Sasco Beach Country Club's parking lot would give the surveillance team a clear view of Alexander's driveway.

Frank and Brenda rang the doorbell several times while waiting for him to open the door. They were just about to leave when the door opened. Alexander looked beat but as usual was able to put on the charm.

"Back so soon, Detectives? I suppose you have a warrant this time."

"No. I'm here to apologize for the other night. I had no right to ask you if I could look around. I really had no reason."

"Well, then if you'll excuse me. I was up late last night and need my beauty rest. You guys woke me up."

"Well, then I apologize again."

As they turned to leave Alexander grabbed Brenda's wrist and said, "My invitation for a photo shoot is still open."

"I'll keep it in mind, Mr. Alexander."

"Mark. Call me Mark."

"I think asshole suits him better," Brenda said when they got back to the car.

*

Alexander picked up his cell phone as soon as they left and called Mya Bates.

"Hello?"

"Hi, Mya. It's Mark. I'm afraid I won't be able to make the party tonight. You'll have to arrange everything for our guests. I don't want you to cancel it on my behalf. Do you think you can handle it?"

"Sure. I don't see why not. What's the problem?"

"I'm kind of busy with something. I may not see you for a couple of days. I promise I'll make it up to you. I've got to run. Bye."

CHAPTER 32

Wednesday 8:00 AM

Lieutenant Nelson called Brenda into his office as soon as he saw her. Frank was already in there and not looking a bit happy.

"What's the matter, Lieutenant?"

"Our surveillance team just got relieved. Alexander didn't leave the property. I don't know how much longer I should waste our resources."

"For Christ's sake, Lieutenant. It's been less than twenty-four hours. Normally we look at somebody for at least seventy-two hours before we pull off."

"Yeah, and normally we would have legal reasons to do it. If the captain finds out he'll be blowing smoke up my ass. I'll give it another twenty-four hours because Frank is backing you on this. If nothing gives with this guy after forty-eight hours I'm pulling them."

"Thanks, Lieutenant," said Brenda. "Anything else?"

"No."

Frank and Brenda left the office and headed for their desks. "Thanks, Frank," said Brenda.

"You're my partner. I'm going to back you. Besides, I think you might be right about that asshole."

"Suppose it doesn't pan out?"

"We'll deal with it."

*

Brenda called Mrs. Pucho to check on Cindee Cox's status while Frank talked to his buddy in New Haven. "Hey, there, Mrs. Pucho, it's Detective Corrino. I was wondering if you heard from Cindee Cox."

"No. I'm worried sick, Detective. I guess you haven't heard anything either. Please find her, Detective. She's really a nice person. She's really nothing like the media makes her out to be."

"Don't worry. I'm sure everything will be all right. I'll call you if we find out anything."

"Thank you, Detective. And I'll call you if she returns."

"Anything?" asked Frank.

"No. She hasn't seen her."

"I might have something. My buddy Ron at the New Haven PD left me a voicemail saying that a homeless woman came forward with some information. I'm trying to get in touch with him. Why don't we run over to the deli and get some lunch?"

"Good idea. I need to get out of the lieutenant's crosshairs."

*

The Center Deli wasn't too busy when Frank and Brenda arrived just before noon. Another ten minutes and they would be waiting in a long line. Frank ordered his usual roast beef and cheese on rye with lettuce, tomato, and mayo. Brenda ordered tuna salad on whole wheat. They both decided to have coffee.

"Frank?"

"Yeah?"

"What if we're wrong about Alexander? Maybe we're out in left field on this one."

"He's all we have. Hopefully he'll make a move soon."

"Yeah. Preferably within the next twenty-four hours."

They shared a soft quiet laugh and continued to eat, momentarily allowing themselves to forget about the case for the moment.

"Are you still dating Crowe?"

"I guess you can call it that. It hasn't become a steady thing, but we're still going out occasionally. Our schedules don't allow us much more than that. "You still married?"

Another laugh, much louder than before, burst from their mouths.

"Our schedules don't allow us much time together either. Is that your cell phone ringing?"

"Yeah."

"Hello."

"Yes. I remember you, Mr. Martin. What can I do for you?"

"I found another DVD in my mailbox."

"Really? When?" asked Brenda.

"Just a few minutes ago. I left it in there. I didn't touch it."

"Then how do you know it's a DVD?"

"Because it's packaged the same as the others."

"You didn't touch it?"

"No."

"Okay. Just leave it there. I'll swing by and pick it up."

Brenda closed her phone and said, "Jay Martin thinks there's another DVD in his mailbox."

They left the remainder of their lunches and told one of the workers that they had to run, pointing to the sandwiches and coffee.

"You want me to wrap them for you, Detectives?" asked one of the deli workers.

"No, no time." yelled Frank, half way out the door.

"Call the lieutenant," Frank said to Brenda as he placed the strobe light on the top of the car. "Tell him to send a car over to Lake Mohegan to look for another body."

CHAPTER 33

Brenda pulled on a pair of latex gloves and retrieved the package from Jay Martin's mailbox. When she returned to the car she carefully opened the package revealing a DVD. Frank began to drive up the driveway to Jay Martin's house.

"What are you doing, Frank?"

"We have to check out the DVD right now to see if we have another victim. I'm sure that pervert Martin won't mind."

"What about fingerprints?"

"Fuck it. None of the others had fingerprints, so I doubt if we'll find any on this DVD."

Before they reached the circular part of the driveway, Frank's cell phone rang and he answered it.

"Shit. I guess that answers that. Okay, we're on our way."

"What's up Frank?"

Frank hesitated before answering. "Cindee Cox. They found her body at the lake."

"Oh no."

*

The scene at Lake Mohegan was all too familiar. The location, the position of the body tied to the tree, the dildos, the nipple jewelry, it was all the same. The body was clean with fresh makeup and decent hair as before. Everything was the same. Three bodies with the same M.O. officially qualified the case as serial. Frank wasn't prepared to go there just yet. Cindee Cox was somebody they had met. That brought it much closer to home.

Brenda spoke first. "I don't know what it is, but something seems different about this one."

"Looks exactly the same to me," answered Frank.

"How could this happen? We're watching Alexander. I guess he isn't the killer after all."

Frank got down on his knees and brought his face close to the victim's vagina. "I don't see a rash of any kind. This one doesn't have the lice rash."

"We can't be sure until the ME shaves her and does a skin scraping," offered Brenda.

"Take a look with your own eyes. She's already shaved pretty clean down there. There's no rash."

Brenda paid no attention to Frank. She was studying the victim's makeup.

"Get a photographer up here with a Polaroid or a digital," she yelled down to the group of uniforms. "I want some head shots." Turning back to Frank she said, "We'll have to get over to her house and find some photos of her, and regrettably, talk to Mrs. Pucho."

"What's going on?" asked Frank.

"Look at her makeup and hair. All the other victims looked like themselves. Whoever made her up wanted her to look like a whore instead of herself. See how her hair is teased? I've never seen a photo of her with teased hair and black eye makeup."

"The lips, fingernails, and toenails are the same as the other victims," said Frank.

"But the hair and makeup are totally different. The bastard must have an accomplice. Somebody else had to complete the delivery of the body while we were watching him." Brenda yelled down to the group of policemen again, "I need forensics back up here. Feel the ground, Frank. The ground was never this wet."

"You're right," he said as he followed the wet ground trail, ending at the water's edge. "It's from the lake. They must be bringing the bodies here by boat."

Frank called the lieutenant asking for a marine crew with a boat and a helicopter to check out the area.

"A helicopter? Are you nuts?"

"I should have thought of it sooner. He's got to be bringing the bodies here by boat. Have them photograph the lake area and all the homes that have access to it, from the air and the boat, including the river that feeds into it. Tell them we are looking for a small boat or a raft of some kind. The transport could even be as simple as a blow-up float."

"What about Alexander?"

"You can take the surveillance off Alexander."

"No shit, Sherlock," snapped the lieutenant. "Unless he's Houdini, you've been barking up the wrong tree."

"Not necessarily. We think he might have an accomplice. I'll fill you in later. Just get me the air and boat support. Make sure they take pictures. I'll catch up with them later."

"Good. You've got a Polaroid, too," Brenda said to the photographer. "Take a few pictures of her face and hair with the Polaroid for me to take with me."

Frank made his way back up from the lake. "Make sure you tell them to check for footprints between here and the lake. I'm going to look around a little, and then we should head over to Mrs. Pucho and give her the bad news."

*

"I'll get into the house while you talk to Mrs. Pucho," Frank said as they pulled in front of Cindee Cox's house.

"Okay."

"This isn't going to be easy, Mrs. Pucho," Brenda said as she told Mrs. Pucho about Cindee Cox's murder. She pulled the Polaroids out of her pocket. "Have you ever seen Ms. Cox with her hair or makeup looking like this?"

She didn't answer at first. She just stared at the photo while wiping tears from her eyes. She finally spoke. "Poor Ms. Cox. No. Never."

"I didn't think so. I read the tabloids now and then, and I've never seen a photograph of her with makeup and hair like this. My partner and I will be next door looking for evidence. Call me if you think of anything that may help us."

"Was that how they killed her? They chocked her with that thing?"

"I'm afraid so, and I am sorry for having to show you these photographs, Mrs. Pucho. There are a lot of sick people out there, and we need all the help we can get to stop this one. If you need someone to talk to, call me."

Brenda found Frank checking the answering machine. "Anything?"

"Messages from a few friends, one from Tony Perceo, and one from Alexander. I suspect he called to throw suspicion off of himself. He's such an asshole. Listen to this," he said as played Alexander's message from the answering machine.

"Hey, Cindee. Where you hiding, babe? I was hoping you'd be

able to come over and spend the night again. I had a great time. I miss you. Give me a call."

"He made the call last night. I assume he guessed we might be watching him, and maybe he thought we had the phones tapped."

"Let me hear the message from Perceo."

"He called two days ago," he said as he pressed the button.

"Hi, sweetheart. It's Tony. I miss you madly. Maybe we can get together and have dinner sometime. Give me a call, please."

"At least he sounds sincere, but I thought he said he wasn't in contact with her. No signs of struggle?" she said as she glanced around the room.

"It's the same in the bedroom," Frank said trying to save her the walk.

"Frank. Look at this."

"Look at what?" he said as he entered the room.

"Here's her makeup."

"She has black, Brenda. She uses black."

"Look at all the makeup, Frank. The black hasn't been touched. Whoever applied her makeup intentionally made it look trashy."

"His jealous girlfriend," they both said at the same time.

"Let's go pay Alexander another visit and get more information about her."

"Wait. He said her name...Mya Bates. Attorney Mya Bates."

"It's too late to check records. Let's head back to the station and talk to one of the prosecutors or a public defender. Somebody must know her."

"I've got to go home for a few hours. I promised Marie I'd spend some quality time with her and the boys tonight. You check her out, and if you need me, call me."

"No problem. Lord knows the world doesn't need another divorced cop."

CHAPTER 34

Wednesday 6:30 PM

Back at headquarters, Brenda caught up with the prosecutor on duty, Attorney Sally Donnelly. Sally tried to look her best, but her best was equal to Brenda's worst. That made Brenda feel superior in spite of Sally's obvious brains. Sally only had good things to say about Mya Bates, however. They were friends outside the courtroom and often had lunch together. Brenda asked her if she ever spoke about her boyfriend.

"David?"

"No. Mark Alexander."

"Oh him. He's her fun date. But David Williams is her main squeeze."

"Williams?"

"Yeah. She met him while she was attending law school. I suspect he helped her out financially with school and setting up her practice. He's a lot older than her, but she says the older the wine the better the taste."

"And what does she say about Alexander?"

"Nothing really. He's her fun date. He's closer to her age, and they do things that David wouldn't want to do."

"Like what?"

Sally blushed but held her cool. "Like going to wild dance clubs in New York and dancing until they close. They like to party."

Dance clubs. Is that what they call places like the Pleasure Chest? Maybe she's a player, too. "Do the men know that the other exists?"

"I don't know. We've only been friendly for about six months."

"Did she ever mention the Pleasure Chest club?"

"No. I don't think so."

"Has she ever asked you about any of our cases?"

"No. She knows better. I don't discuss our cases with anybody on the outside. Why are you so interested in her?"

"I need to ask her a few questions about a case. Do you know where she lives?"

"She lives in Greenwich. I have her cell phone number. It's 230-227-8123."

Brenda went to her desk and dialed the number several times, but nobody answered. Not willing to call it a night she decided to do something bizarre. She called Mark Alexander to arrange for her photo session. He told her he didn't work at night, but she insisted. He said he would make an exception for her. She agreed to be at his house at nine o'clock. He told her to dress sexy and bring a bathing suit. He would provide anything else she might need.

Brenda headed home to shower and get dressed for her photo shoot. She tried to reach Frank on his cell phone but it went directly into his voicemail. *He must have it off, damn it. Quality family time, my ass.* She left him a voicemail explaining her plan to get into Alexander's house to look for some DNA evidence to tie him to the murderers.

Next she called Darren to explain what she was up to. He tried to talk her out of it, but she'd already made up her mind. She was going to take the asshole down one way or another. As a back up she would call him no later than eleven o'clock. If he didn't hear from her by then he was to call Frank for backup immediately.

*

Wednesday, 8:15 PM

Brenda took a quick shower and tried on a few bathing suits looking for something sexy but nothing too revealing. She settled on a black bikini that provided plenty of coverage for her ass. *Wait a minute. What am I thinking? I'm not parading around in my bikini for that pervert.* She threw the bathing suit back in the drawer and put on a shiny red bra and matching panty. *That will do just fine.* She picked her new red and gold Asian-styled suit. The jacket buttoned in the front with a deep V-neck. It has three-quarter sleeves and a slit skirt that screamed legs. She bought it to wear on her next date with Darren. *Oh well.* A pair of red FM's completed the outfit. She finished applying her makeup, being sure to wear bright red lipstick and nail polish.She strapped her backup weapon, a derringer, high on her inner thigh, at the edge of her panties. *If he reaches up there I'll blow his fucking hand off.* She checked her weapon in her purse and headed out the door before she lost her nerve.

Brenda tried unsuccessfully to contact Frank again on both his home and cell phones on her way to Sasco Hill Road. *He has them both off. Quality family time, my ass. More like quality screwing time!* Brenda arrived at Alexander's precisely at nine o'clock.

CHAPTER 35

Mark answered the door wearing blue jeans and a collared, three-button, white cotton shirt with Celebrity Sightings embroidered on it.

"Hi, Detective Corrino, or can I call you Brenda tonight?"

"I prefer 'Detective.'"

"Come in. How about Brenda, just for tonight?"

"Okay, just for tonight."

"That's a great outfit, and I love the color."

"Thanks."

"Follow me."

"This is my great room. We'll talk in here about the shoot before we start."

Brenda felt a little uneasy being in a room with a hot tub and mirrored walls. "I thought you had a studio here."

"Relax," Alexander replied with a smile. "It's in there," motioning towards a door on the opposite side of the room. "It's in the perfect location near the hot tub and pool. Most of my photo shoots spill over to both for some nice sexy water shots."

Mark opened a bottle of Cabernet Sauvignon and poured them each a glass. "I sense you are very tense about doing this," Mark said as he handed her a glass. "This usually helps to ease the mind and relax the soul."

"I'll need more than this," she said while looking at the glass.

"Drink up Brenda. I've got plenty."

They sipped the wine as Mark explained about the type of photos he was expecting to produce. Some would show her as bold and sophisticated. Some would show her as sexy. In any case she'd look hot.

"Good. I want to look hot."

"Did you bring a bathing suit?"

"No. I decided to wait and see how this session goes. If I like the photos I'll do a bathing suit session another time."

Mark laughed to himself. *She's worried about me seeing her in a bathing suit.* "Let me finish setting up my camera and lighting while you relax with the wine," he said while walking through the studio door. "Feel free to soak your feet in the tub," he yelled from the studio.

Brenda took the opportunity to look around. The room had a beautiful bar with plenty of cabinets and drawers. She found more matches from the Pleasure Chest and several boxes of colored and flavored lubricated prophylactics.

Flavored? That's a new one. She also found a photo album of many naked women who mostly appeared to be stoned. Some of them looked like they didn't even know that the camera was there. Some were taken in the hot tub and others by the pool. Many photographs of naked women taking a shower, all from the same angle, also filled several pages. *He must have a camera hidden above a shower somewhere.* The very last page of the album was a printout of a website advertising nude prints of celebrity and celebrity wannabes. *That asshole. He must sell them on the Internet, too. I wonder if the women know.*

"Find anything interesting?" Mark said as he reentered the great room.

Brenda pretended to be looking out the window at the pool. "How early in the season do you open your pool?"

"On April Fools Day every year. I'm ready if you are."

"Sure. Let's do it. First I need the bathroom."

"There are two down the hall past the kitchen and one upstairs in my bedroom. If you want good light to touch up your makeup, use the one upstairs."

"Good idea. I can kill two birds with one stone," she said with a smirk while walking in the direction that he was pointing.

"Love those heels, Detective."

She found her way to the stairs and his bedroom, locking the door behind her. The only thing unusual about the bedroom was the mirror built in to the top of the bed's canopy frame. She pulled open the drawer of the nightstand and found several dildos and vibrators. One appeared to be similar to the murder weapon but not an exact match. The search of the contents of a large dresser proved to be fruitless. *No Rohypnol.* She searched the white tiled bathroom but came up empty except for a hairbrush. She pulled off the few hairs that it had trapped, stuck them in a tissue, and into her purse. She also noted that the shower was probably the same as the one pictured in the album. She quickly applied fresh lipstick, flushed the toilet, and headed back downstairs to the studio.

"I guess I'm more nervous than I thought."

"No problem. Stand in front of that white screen so I can take a few test shots."

He took three photos from different angles with a Polaroid camera and set them aside while they developed. "Would you like another glass of wine for your nerves?"

"Do you have any merlot?" Brenda said. "I didn't like the other wine very much."

"Sure." *Smart lady. She's afraid I may have doped up the bottle while she was upstairs.*

He opened the bottle right in front of her and took two glasses out from a small hutch behind him. "New bottle, new glasses."

She walked over to where he was pouring, trying to see if he might possibly slip something into her wine. She took the glass closest to him, just to be safe. He took the other glass and said, "I propose a toast to the prettiest detective I've ever photographed." *One I'm going to enjoy fucking too!* He touched his glass to hers, smiling like a kid on Christmas morning.

Brenda couldn't stop herself from laughing at his little pun.

"Let's start by you sitting on this chair with your legs crossed. It's one of my favorite tease shots and very hot. We'll try a few with the wine glass and a few without it."

Brenda complied with his request and sat on the chair with her legs crossed.

"Detective. I mean Brenda. I'm afraid your gun is showing," he said as he pointed towards her thighs. "Do you want it to show?"

"Sure. Why not? I'm a hot, sexy woman detective, aren't I?" she said as she unbuttoned her jacket and let it fall open revealing her red bra. How this? Hot enough?"

"Perfect."

CHAPTER 36

Thursday 12:30 AM

Brenda dreamt of making love to Darren. They made wild passionate love at her beach house, in the hot tub, on the bed, and on the floor. They took liberties with each other like never before, both willing to taste forbidden fruit. Wild, wicked, passionate sex. The kind of hot sex that can leave you with a good hurt that stays with you for several days. Then her dream turned into her worst nightmare. She woke up and found she was bound to a strange bed in a strange, stark white room, and naked. The ceiling was covered with large, poster-sized photographs of her. The photos showed her naked except for her weapon strapped to her thigh. Some of the photos showed the weapon in her mouth and others showed it stuck in her anus. She was confused and dazed. She began to notice her body ached. She tried to speak but her throat was too dry to allow audible sounds. She forced her head up to look around and she caught a glimpse of her breasts. Her nipples were pierced with gold jewelry. The gold jewelry was the same that she saw on the murder victims. Reality set in. She was about to become the next murder victim.

*

Darren tried to contact Frank after not hearing from Brenda at eleven o'clock, but there was only his voicemail. He didn't know what to do. *I'm a doctor, not a cop.* He left a message on Frank's cell and house phones before going to Alexander's house. Brenda's car was not in the driveway. The house was dark and no one answered to the doorbell. Armed with a baseball bat, he broke a window and climbed inside. He found a light switch and illuminated the foyer, and walked down the hall until he found another. He could hear what sounded like a hot tub bubbling in the room that he entered next, again turning on another light switch. The room was a bit messy like the aftermath of a party. Two wine glasses partial filled rested near the hot tub. In the adjoining room a woman's red and gold jacket and skirt, red bra, and panties lay scattered about. He saw several more used wine glasses and three opened bottles of wine. He started to yell out Brenda's name but decided to check the upstairs first. Another messy room. The bed was unmade and littered with sex toys. The shower and the bathroom sinks were wet.

"Brenda?" Darren screamed loudly. He ran downstairs and back into the great room. Darren screamed louder "Brenda?"

"Drop the bat and put your hands up. Don't move," Frank said while pointing his weapon at Darren.

"Frank it's me, Darren Crowe. Brenda's not here."

"Is Alexander here?" Frank asked as he lowered his weapon.

"I don't think so."

He led Frank to the great room and the studio.

"Do you recognize the clothes?" Frank asked while pointing towards the scattered items. "You think they're Brenda's?"

"No, but they could be hers," he said while picking up the jacket and reading the label. "I think it's her size. This could be hers."

"Hey, don't touch anything else." Frank examined the wine bottles and glasses, being careful not to disturb the evidence.

"Shit."

"What is it?"

"You tell me, Doc," Frank said as he motioned him over to a small bar and pointed at a syringe laying on a lower shelf.

Darren bent over to get a closer look and sniff the needle. "It's odorless. I don't know what it is."

Frank held the corks from the wine bottles up to the light. "He used it to lace the wine. He stuck it through the cork. He must of ground up Rohypnol, dissolved it in some liquid, and injected it into the bottle. Do you think that would work?"

"I don't see why not," Darren said as he gave the syringe another look. "I think you're right. I can't say that it's Rohypnol, but I can see that something was ground up and added to a liquid solution. Some of the solid particles have settled."

"Oh, fuck no," Frank said as he picked up a Polaroid photo off the floor.

"What is it?"

He handed him the photo of Brenda wearing the discarded clothes as he called headquarters and filled in the detectives on duty. He told them to get a warrant and send over a team to tear the house apart. He also directed them to gather the photos taken earlier by the helicopter and meet him at Lake Mohegan with as many policemen that were available.

*

Thursday 01:30 AM

"Alexander," Brenda said as loudly as she could. "Where are you? Your little game is over. Do you think I went to your house without telling anybody? Without backup? Half of the Fairfield Police Department is on their way here. Alexander? Answer me, you bastard!"

Alexander observed her through the two-way mirrored glass walls, same as he had observed and recorded the others. *The police will go to Sasco Hill Road. We aren't in Fairfield.* He wanted her to break down and cry or beg like the others, but she wouldn't give him the satisfaction. He entered the white room and said, "Hello, Detective."

"Where's your mask?"

He ignored her question and cupped a breast, pulling it upward so she could see what he did to her nipple. "You like my present?"

"Fuck you!"

"And I thought you were the type of girl that would appreciate jewelry."

"If you touch me again I'll make sure they let me kill you when they get here."

"Touch you? I'm afraid it's too late, Detective. We already made love every way possible. In fact I think we may have invented some new ones. You are quite talented in that regard. Do you like your photographs?" he said as he pointed to the ceiling. "I think that little pistol is a real turn on. Did you see the one with the barrel in your ass? That's my favorite!"

"Fuck you...you pervert."

"Unfortunately there isn't enough time for me to share you

with my horny friends. I would have enjoyed watching you squirm. Mya and I did our best to satisfy your every wish and desire." He slowed ran his fingers down through her pubic hair while she tried to squirm away. "Did we satisfy you or do you need more sex?" He smiled when she stiffened below his fingering touch.

"Why are you doing this? We know everything about you and your team of homeless rapists. You and Mya will rot in jail if you're lucky."

"Women think they can just ignore me and dismiss me as some inferior creature. They turn me on with their sexy poses and sexual powers and then turn it off and turn me down like some dog. I'm a man and a man has basic needs."

"Does a man's basic needs include murder?"

"Enough talk," he said as he covered her face with a feathered mask and turned to leave the room. "By the way, you won't be rescued. We're not at Sasco Hill anymore."

Brenda welcomed the mask because it hid her trepidation and tears.

CHAPTER 37

Frank, Darren, and six policemen gathered at the Lake Mohegan parking lot at approximately two AM. Frank spread the aerial photographs taken by the helicopter on the hood of a car so everyone could see them. Six homes were within three hundred feet of the lake with access to the water and another five within eight hundred feet. Eight were in Fairfield and three in Easton. None of the photos revealed any boats. Frank explained the situation to them, making sure they understood it was one of their own in trouble. He assigned each policeman a house to check in Fairfield. After they cleared the house they were to investigate the two remaining Fairfield homes. He asked them to speak up if anyone didn't feel comfortable going in without backup. No one spoke up. They knew Brenda's life was on the line. He gave them a brief description of Alexander. He told them to assume Alexander was armed because he probably had Brenda's weapons. Darren and Frank took the Easton homes.

A report that accommodated the photos included a map from the Wetlands Commission showing well and sewer lines that were required when the houses were built. Frank had a hunch based on the map. The three Easton homes used to have drywells in the rear of the property near the lake. They had to abandon the drywells and septic systems when the lake was created and connect the plumbing into the town facilities out in the street. These homes were originally built in the early twentieth century, before the use of conventional pipes for drainage. The waste water reached the drywells through a channel made of stones, surrounded by earth. Often those channels were made large enough for a man to walk through in a hunched position to perform maintenance.

"Maybe that's how he gets the body to the water without being visible," Frank said to Darren as he pointed to the map.

"Why do that? He could carry the body to the lake and then put it in a boat. Nobody is going to see him at three o'clock in the morning."

"Why should he risk being seen if he doesn't have to?" Frank said.

"Maybe the channel is partially under the lake," they both said simultaneously.

"I'll leave you at this house," Frank said pointing on the map and to the house closest to them in Easton. "I'll take the farthest house. If those are clear we converge on the house in the middle. Look through the windows first. If you don't see anything out of the ordinary bang on the front door. If the lights don't come on or nobody answers the door after you count to ten, break in and find the basement. If I'm right about the old drainage channel, he'll have her in the basement."

The house that Darren checked had two elderly people living in it. He briefly questioned them and found that they hadn't seen or heard anything out of the ordinary tonight or any night. He did find out that the house next door didn't have full-time occupants.

They never met the owner but understood that a young man inherited the house from his aunt several years ago. The house was set quite a distance back from the street, so it was hard to see when people were there. Darren apologized for the intrusion and began to let himself out when the old man suddenly remembered something. When he had gotten up about one o'clock this morning to use the bathroom, he noticed that there was a light on in that house, but only for a few minutes.

*

Brenda struggled to free herself from the restraints, but couldn't. The marine-grade rope was made of heavy stock and the weight alone made it difficult to maneuver her hands and feet. *I've got to do something. He'll be back to kill me soon. I've got to delay him. Buy some time. Think damn it. Think!*

When Alexander returned, he was wearing the all-too-familiar Mickey Mouse mask. The sight of it sending shivers throughout Brenda's body, causing her to tremble uncontrollably. *Think ,damn it. Think!* He laid a ten-inch dildo between her breasts and slid it up and down tauntingly. She knew her death was near.

"I think you're right, Mark. I didn't have enough sex. I don't remember enjoying your huge dick inside me. You know I'm just a big slut. How about doing me again, right now? Please, Mark. Let me enjoy you one last time."

He hesitated before answering, conjuring the scene in his head. "I wish there was time. I'd really enjoy having you while you're tied up and cognizant. Unfortunately, there isn't time."

"You said we aren't in Sasco Hill anymore. Nobody knows where we are then, right? So what's the rush? Come on. Get your girlfriend over here, too. I want both of you, right here and now."

Alexander thought about what she had said. *Surely she's right. Those asshole cops don't have a clue of where we are.*

"Come on, Mark, take it out. Let me see that big beautiful thing again."

Alexander left the room without answering her. Brenda was doing what she had to do. What she was trained to do. She was buying time at any cost. Selling her soul to the devil in hopes of surviving to see another day to make Alexander pay with his life for the horrendous murders he committed.

Frank will figure it out and find me. He's smart. He just needs more time. He's my partner. He'll find me. I've got to buy more time.

*

Darren was at the front door of the stone house that sat back far from the road. It was dark both inside and out. Frank was nowhere in sight. He pressed the doorbell button and didn't hear it make a sound. He knocked on the door with his baseball bat and counted to ten. Still no response. He looked toward the house that Frank went to, hoping to see Frank heading his way. *Shit. Where is he? Maybe he found them. Maybe he needs help. No. Stick to the game plan.* Darren broke a window and let himself in. His eyes were partially accustomed to the dark outdoors, and within a few seconds he was able to see well enough inside the house to notice a faint light glowing from underneath a door.

He opened the door and descended the stairs as quietly as possible. As he reached the bottom he could see that the light came from the far corner of the basement. He cautiously headed that way until he found the room that held Brenda captive. He looked through the glass and saw a naked woman wearing a feathered mask and photos of Brenda on the ceiling. She was tied to the bed with a thick rope. He quickly looked around the basement for Alexander, but it appeared that he was alone. He entered the brightly lit room and pulled off her mask.

"Brenda. Are you okay?"

"Darren. Untie me before he comes back," she said as tears began to fill up her eyes.

"Was it Alexander?" he asked as he leaned over her and began to untie her left hand, feeling the nipple jewelry scrape his arm. He looked down at her breasts and saw the dildo resting there. Instinctively, he grabbed it and threw it towards the corner, realizing for the first time that the inside of the windows were mirrored.

"Yes. Please hurry."

Darren started to untie her right hand when Alexander came charging into the room, bashing Darren's head with the baseball bat that he foolishly had left outside the door. He hit him a few times to make sure that he wouldn't be interfering again.

"Stop. Don't kill him!"

"Shut up, slut," he replied as he slapped her hard across the face. "You're all the same. You want sex on your terms only. Not this time, and not ever again. I'm calling the shots. You can't order me to have sex anymore. Those days are over. I decide who and when. Not you. Where's the dildo?" he asked as he wrapped his hand around her throat and began to choke her. She didn't reply. He looked around the room, spotted it on the floor and picked it up.

"It's a pity that I have to rush this now," he said as he placed the dirty dildo into her mouth. "Mya and I were going to grant you your wish, but there's no time now." He began to push it down her throat when a shot rang out and broke the two-way mirrored glass. As he turned, Frank entered the room like a wild animal and grabbed Alexander, throwing him against the wall. They exchanged a few punches, but he was no match for Frank. Frank beat him until he was unconscious and then turned his attention to Brenda.

"Are you hurt?" he asked as he grabbed her right hand to untie it.

"Frank!" she screamed as she saw Alexander's girlfriend Mya Bates through the hole where the glass used to be. She pointed a gun at Frank and ordered him to put down his gun. He did as he was told and placed his weapon on Brenda's stomach. She ordered him to move away from Brenda. Once he did that she entered the room and attempted to revive Alexander, while keeping her pistol aimed at Frank.

That's when Brenda made her move, grabbing Frank's weapon off her belly with her left hand and in one fluid motion, she shot Bates pointblank in the left side of her head, killing her instantly. Frank was covered from the waist down with Mya Bates brain matter and blood, but it didn't faze him in the least.

After Frank untied Brenda she stood over Alexander's listless body and kicked him in the face with tremendous force, ripping his nose off to one side. Then she kicked him in the groin, not once, not twice, but three times. Frank pulled her back to stop her, wrapping his arms around her cold, naked, trembling body, drawing her tightly against him. He could feel the coldness of her body through his clothes, so he took off his shirt and wrapped it around her shoulders.

Brenda shivered as she said, "That was for Alana, Candie, and Cindee."

EPILOGUE

Tuesday, September 7, 2004

Detective Brenda Corrino never returned to work. Nor did she acknowledge her accolades from the police commissioner or First Selectman Ken Flatto for her involvement in the capture of serial killer Mark Alexander and his accomplice Mya Bates. Instead she spent her days in psychiatric counseling and group therapy. She was aware that she needed to heal and put her brutal rape and abduction behind her in order to help put Alexander and Bates away for life or hopefully death. The trial was scheduled to start during the winter of 2005 and she was expected to be the star witness for the prosecution.

She was searching for the toughness that drove her to pursue Alexander. She was reaching for the strength that drove her to become the first woman homicide detective in the Fairfield Police Department. Yet, they continue to elude her. They told her the sleepless nights filled with nightmares would end. They hadn't. They told her that she would once again enjoy the intimacy of a man. She couldn't.

Doctor Darren Crowe made a full recovery from his injuries and was back at work in the Medical Examiner's office. He longed for the day that Brenda no longer needed therapy. He, too, wanted Brenda to enjoy the closeness of a man. He wanted to tell her that he loved her. He wanted to hold her in his arms and kiss her hard, feeling her breasts swell with desire against his chest. She had no desire.

He longed to share a glass of wine while they soak in her hot tub, sharing stories of the day's events. When they spoke she was evasive and distant. When they hugged it was like brother and sister. A kiss on the cheek or forehead replaced the long, sensual kisses that led to the most passionate love-making he ever experienced. Her doctors told him to be patient. They said she was tough and would figure out a way to overcome the trauma. It agitated him deeply because he was a doctor, yet he couldn't help her get over the ordeal.

As for Detective Frank Gianni, all was well. Being splattered in the face with Mya Bate's brains was a good thing to him. That meant that his partner saved his life. It meant that the killings would stop. Even though Brenda had been drugged and raped multiple times, she was still able to think clearly to finish freeing her left hand and was able to muster up the strength and courage to shoot Mya Bates without hesitation. She knew what Frank expected her to do the moment he placed his weapon on her body. He positioned it so she could easily grab it with her left hand and fire in one smooth motion. She saved both their lives. He missed her. He wanted her. He wanted his partner back.

An investigation into Alexander's childhood provided answers to obvious questions. It appeared that Alexander's mother forced him to have sex with her friends while she watched through a two-way mirror, often recording the act with a Polaroid camera. It started when he was twelve years old. It ended four years later when she died in a car accident. His aunt took him in and upon her death he inherited the Fairfield and Easton properties. He used the photography business as a front for sexual encounters. Some were consensual but many were not.

Since Alexander's arrest, several women had come forward and admitted that they were victims of his sexual abuse as well. They were the lucky ones. They were allowed to live.

Frank was offered and accepted the newly created position of Regional Special Investigator for Fairfield and New Haven Counties. This position would report to Lieutenant Colonel Vincent McNarly, Commanding Officer of the Bureau of Criminal Investigations of the Connecticut State Police Department's Field Operations. His office would be located at the Mulcahy Complex in Meriden. The primary function of the Bureau of Criminal Investigations was to perform specialized department investigations in the areas of serial murders, narcotics, organized crime, central criminal intelligence, firearms trafficking, gang activity, fugitive investigations, and electronic surveillance. Frank would commandeer investigations from local police departments in Fairfield or New Haven Counties concerning serial crimes, whether facultative or de facto, at the request of the governor's Office, when deemed necessary to accelerate an investigation.

Printed in the United States
63332LVS00001B/1-99

9 781424 139453